SCALE:
SEEKER OF ABSOLUTION

IAN YOUNG

Upscale Games & Funky Fresh Publishing

 ISBN: 979-8-9931624-0-9 (print)

Cover Art by Theo Stai & Luke Waldoch

Book design by Ian Young (Atticus)

Upscale Games in assoc. with Funky Fresh Publishing

Made in Minnesota, printed in the United States of America

contact@upscale.games

ALSO BY IAN YOUNG

NOVELS

The Automaton

Ashen Light

SHORT STORY COLLECTIONS

Darkness Unknown: Tales of the Terrific and Terrifying

.

To Sharon
She hates dragons.

CONTENTS

Foreword

Have you ever even read a book's foreword? What a boring pile of crap right? *Well, prepare to read about awesome dragons and other slightly less awesome characters, because we have to have contrast for more interesting character development!*

This book is brought to you by ~~Arby's~~ a lot of tedious nitpicking and stress! Also mostly by Ian. He's the man. No, he isn't a local area network. It's an I not an l. Ha! Good luck deciphering that one. Is this where I say how awesome Ian is? I mean as far as network connections go, it was great for playing Halo with some pals...but the writer guy is pretty cool too.

We found Ian in the trash at a convention that was run by Gerald Ford, or some horrible simulacrum of him at least. He was like the one sad discarded nugget you stare at and contemplate in the trash when you're super hungry, and then when you go to eat it, you put it in your mouth only to realize *it was a golden nugget the whole time!* Super great guy. Fun to work with, writes stuff goodly, and likes long walks on the beach. Also likes scritchies behind the ear sometimes, and can't pass up a good ol' chicken biscuit. Wait... Never mind, that last one is about my cat. (I mean, who doesn't like ear scritchies?)

This book is supposed to be fun. If you aren't having fun reading it, please throw it in the trash, or send it to someone you hate, because if you hate them, they are probably a fun person who would enjoy this book more than you. Anyway, we hope you enjoy reading about one of the coolest dragons in the *SCALE* universe. There's also a physical AND a digital card game in this universe, we are also working on a TV show, another book, a board game, a line of mid-sized SUV's, affordable healthcare, a signature roast beef sandwich, and now you should just pretend I wrote some more funny stuff here, laugh loudly and slap your knee, then look around and tell everyone else around you how great this book is. Thanks for reading!

Love,
Theo

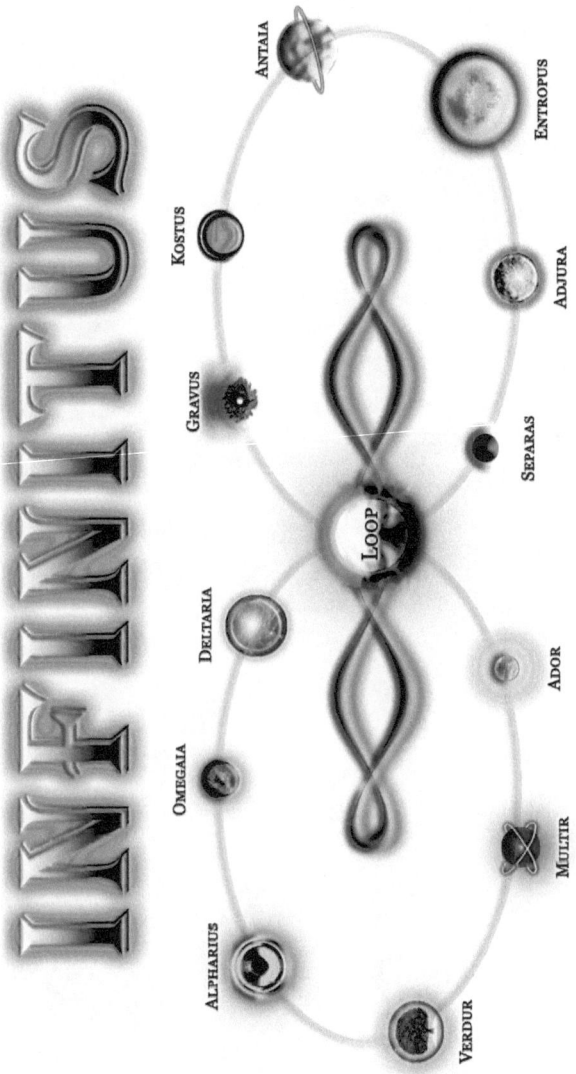

Loss of
What Makes
Us, Us

A figure stood upon the high, ragged cliff as a harsh wind violently whipped their ebony cloak. Far below, the green seas roiled under the jaundice sky of Entropus, one of the twelve planets of Infinitus. The figure waited. Time was irrelevant. It wasn't a matter of if, but when.

The waters below the cliffs eddied and swirled, frothed and foamed. If the figure had a face, it'd smile. If it had a body, it'd tremble. They had come and they had found their quarry.

From the waters of Entropus burst forth the dragon. He surged up the side of the ragged, stone cliffs and flew at the figure. He circled twice above in the sky, then soared past before settling on the ground in front of the mysterious newcomer. The dragon's eyes shone–cold and ice blue. A thousand needle-like fangs lined its mouth, showing their only purpose was violence and wrath. His spiny scales clicked together as the dragon continuously coiled over itself, towering in its glory over the figure.

"Null." The figure's voice was a chorus of raspy whispers.

The dragon heard this, despite the distance. His body stilled in the air, then started again, growing closer, circling. "You are not human..." he said, studying. "You are not Valkyr, and you certainly are no dragon. No, you are something entirely different, and far more...interesting. Yes, far more interesting. What are you, I wonder?"

The figure spread wide their arms. "We are The Seeker."

"The Seeker?" The dragon laughed. "And, what is it you seek?"

"That which makes you, you."

Again, Null found his amusement. "You know my name, I presume?"

"We do."

"Then your mission has been for nothing!"

The Seeker's hand moved slowly for the edges of their cloak, and pulled it back. There was no body. Instead, floating in a mass of black smoke sat a dazzling stone no larger than a human heart. It was as dark as The Seeker's vestments, but shone with every color of light's visible spectrum. The great dragon's eye gleamed, transfixed.

"Is that a—"

"Yes," the chorus replied.

The stone gleamed in the light, and Null's wrath exploded as the stone's effects took hold of him. The dragon writhed, spun in and around itself, churning the ground underneath as tendrils of pain seeped into his body. The Seeker merely watched and waited. Null reared up and bellowed, echoing his wrath over the cliffs. The dragon fell on his side with a pathetic thud, heaving his massive lungs.

"What..." Null asked, gasping for air, "have you done?"

The Seeker raised a ghostly hand. It snapped a finger and a small purple flame lit upon its middle fingertip.

Magic.

"That's impossible," the dragon whispered. "I am...Null."

"You," the chorus of The Seeker whispered back, "are nothing."

1

NEVER BET
AGAINST A
DRAGON

In one of the magical dead zones of the planet Separas, where creatures of all types lived, the streets were silent save for the thumping of music inside the concrete buildings. Of all the dance clubs in Xeresis City, The Big Sauce was the *it* club of the cycle. It opened three days ago and would likely be shut down in the next two. Beasts and creatures of all shapes and sizes squeezed together, moving as one to the pulsating rhythm and frenetic lights. Compared to most dragons, a seven foot tall, bipedal, black and blue scaled dragon was easily missed in the crowd.

He sat down in a dark corner booth in the back across from a large, fish-like Gorgian male—one could tell by the bright green fins behind its ears. Fawning over him with spiny fingers were two, equally fishy female companions. A third female sat by as well. The dragon could tell they were female because of the dark green fins behind their ears. It was that easy. Get it wrong, and he'd feel the wrath of the Gorgians. He was fairly confident he wouldn't feel that tonight.

The dragon shuffled a glowing deck of cards and placed it in front of the fish.

"Take the top three cards," he said.

"I no trust. You shuffled." The Gorgian's deep, heavily accented voice boomed over the Sythropian trance music.

"It doesn't matter because you're going to show me the cards anyway." The dragon took the top three and laid them on the table face up. "Now, I know the cards, and you know the cards. Take them in your hand so I can't see. Choose one to keep, then shuffle the others back into the deck."

Bemused, the Gorgian did as directed.

"Now, I bet you I can tell you which card of the three you kept, simply by asking you three, completely unrelated questions. Understood?"

The Gorgian let out what the dragon hoped was a laugh, otherwise he was choking.

"What are terms?"

"Smart." The dragon smiled. "Very smart. You know, I've heard Gorgians are clever. Here are the terms: if I guess correctly..." he reached into his back pocket and extracted a pair of humming binding cuffs. "You come with me. Nicely, quietly."

Another choking laugh came from the Gorgian. "And if *you* guess wrong..." the male said and snapped his fingers.

The female to his right produced a snazzium-plated plasma pistol and handed it to the male.

"I kill you?"

The dragon smiled again. "This makes the game that much more interesting, doesn't it? Alright. I get three questions. You answer truthfully, too. Got it?"

The Gorgian pointed inward, "What me? Always truthful. Understand."

"Excellent! Question one: What's the name of the..." He squinted in the dim light, staring hard at the fins behind the ears of the creature sitting next to the male. "Lovely lady...that gave you the pistol?"

The Gorgian's downturned fish jaw dropped. "Uh...Jova."

"Good. And you like her?"

"Yeah, she okay, I guess."

Jova crossed her arms and huffed. The other female patted her back.

"That's too bad." Before the Gorgians could blink their double eye-lids, the dragon had reached over and bound Jova's wrist firmly in a binding cuff. The other cuff he clamped to himself.

"Wait, just moment!" The male Gorgian yelled, briny spittle flying from his mouth.

"Oh, right, sorry. I still have a third question—"

"No, what you do with Jova?"

"She has quite the bounty on her head, don't you Jova? Arms dealing? Shouldn't have shown off such a pretty toy." The dragon pointed to the shiny pistol reflecting the multitude of colored lights of the dance club like a prism in sunlight.

"I hate constabularies!" The male raised the pistol.

Before it was fully brought to bear, the dragon seized the barrel, ripped the weapon out of the Gorgian's hand, flip-turned the gun, and pointed it in between the eyes where he hoped the brain was. Slowly, the male brought his hands up. The dragon scoffed, lowered the weapon, then thought better of it, slamming the butt of the pistol across the Gorgian's arrogant face.

"First off, I'm not a constabulary. I do this for the credits, not for the justice. Second, I'm a dragon, you imbecile. You pose no threat to me, *even* armed. Come on Jova, we've got a date." The dragon turned back to the male Gorgian who was rubbing his cheek. "Don't look so cross, you still have two ladies to take care of you."

"That one is my son!" the Gorgian yelled, spittle flinging from his mouth.

"Oh." The dragon squinted again in the light. "Oh yeah, I see it now. Well, time to get going then." The dragon reached down, grabbed his deck of cards, and kept the pistol for good measure.

"By the way," he said over his shoulder, "the card you kept was the queen of forks."

Then, he escorted the bounty out of the club as curious eyes followed them out.

That's how I got my name.

Query.

I ask questions.

It isn't my real name, of course. My real name is utterly unpronounceable in its native Draconic by anyone or anything other than dragons, and most still never use it. Even some of the minor dragons have trouble saying it, so they stick with Query.

A lot of my prey are arrogant. Arrogant and dumb. That card trick works every time. They let their guard down, think they're about to win, and that's when I strike.

For those wondering how I did my card trick, a magician never reveals his secrets. I don't give a grunk, so I'll tell ya. My trusty deck is see-through. Only to me. Just a little bit of magic that has saved me over the years. Plus it's hilarious to mess with people like that. You should have seen that dumb Gorgian's face when I told him the correct card.

Jova was a tough one. The thing is, all Gorgians look alike under dim lights and there's nothing dimmer than a dance club. Unfortunately for me, The Big Sauce was the place I knew she'd be tonight. She'd been caught a few times for arms trafficking, but nothing stuck. It wasn't until she met that sideways-buttfaced male Gorgian that she started going full-time. The credits were just too tempting. Something I could relate to. Tonight, I just needed the positive ID.

With our cuffed hands concealed behind her back, I led her out of the club through the back doors, the same ones bouncers used when giving the rowdier patrons the heave-ho. The ones where they kindly asked you to leave by pommeling you senseless until you no longer could stand up on your own. I absolutely wouldn't know from experience. I crumpled the pistol in my hand and threw it in the trash. It was junk anyway.

That's when I saw her, standing at the outlet of the trash-ridden alleyway. I wasn't totally sure, but I confirmed it the moment she said my name.

"Query."

I couldn't believe it, but it was her.

A small girl, human, smudged with dirt and wrapped in rags. Dark hair flicked out from underneath her hood and whipped in the wind, despite the air being still and stale. She looked more at home in the alley than the random bits of trash did. As if on cue, those bits of trash and detritus moved away from her toward dumpsters or into piles of their own.

"Let her go." Her voice was deep, ethereal, mature. It didn't match her looks.

I turned to the Gorgian then back to the child. "Oh come on! I've been tracking her for a Separian cycle. Do you know how long that is?"

The child crossed her arms. "Yes, I created it."

"I need this."

"And I need you." Her eyes narrowed. "Let her go."

Dammit. I really couldn't say no.

I turned back to my bounty. "Jova, you have no idea just how lucky you are." I undid her binding cuffs and pushed her away.

"You won't find me again," she said, casting a smirk in my direction.

I returned the smile. "Oh, I will."

She ran off deep into the seedy alleyway. There went a ten-thousand credit bounty, practically skipping like she got a second chance at life. I *will* find her again.

I turned back to the child, but she was no longer there. Instead a towering, elegantly spiked and steel-armored dragon stood before me. She unfurled her wings which spanned wider than her eight foot height. Her tail coiled around her body. She was beautiful, she was ancient, she was divine. To be fair, she was a deity. Anyone walking past still saw the human child.

I bowed my head. "Exodus! To what do I owe this grand honor?"

"Query, the realm is in imbalance."

"The realm is always in imbalance. What else is new?"

Her eyes flared. "Such flippancy! Even in the face of an Ancient?"

I winced. She was right. Sometimes it's hard to turn it off and frankly, I was still upset about losing my bounty.

"My apologies, your worship." That seemed to abate some of her anger.

"Something has happened to your dragon brethren."

"What is it?"

"See for yourself."

As annoying as that is, okay, fine. I have some magic abilities that help me do my job. One of these abilities lets me see where certain creatures are at any given time. Mostly, I can see the location of any dragon in Infinitus. Not super helpful, but if I need answers, I know where to find them.

I looked around, seeing if anyone was watching. Nothing suspicious about a dragon speaking to a little human girl who barely makes it up to his knee. I closed my eyes, concentrated, and opened my hand. I can feel when it appears, a small pink scrying orb that is my link into the aether. Like a tugging, a tethering of my mind to another world. The realm within the realm. It connects me to my dragon brothers and sisters. My mind can sift through them all.

Sure enough, something was off with some of them.

"Good news, they aren't dead."

"How do you know?"

"For example, you appear incredibly bright because you are standing right next to me. If I look to the opposite side of Infinitus—someone like Alpha looks incredibly dim. If a dragon were dead, I wouldn't see anything at all. But some of these dragons...it's like I'm seeing a shell or a ghost of them. There's no light coming from them at all, but they're there. It's odd."

Then she said what I was hoping she wouldn't.

"Find out what is happening."

Double dammit.

"Why me? I'm just a bounty hunter. Why not have Alpha or anyone else deal with it? I'm small-time."

Exodus flexed her wings. "Because this isn't just a 'what' problem, but a 'who' problem. Someone is doing this."

"How do you know?"

She smiled, ignoring his question. "I need you to track and destroy whoever it is. Find the one who calls themselves The Seeker. Capture or destroy them."

I crossed my arms. "And what if I say no?"

She picked at one of her talons with her thumb. "And what if I eviscerate you and feed you to the rotbirds? Hm? But then you wouldn't be able to help me, would you? So, I ply your hand with the promise of rewards."

"Rewards, eh?"

"Yes, of course you'd be compensated for saving the realm. Oh yes, Query, you'd be a savior. People would love you, fawn over you, celebrate your name." She made a mocking gesture with each point.

"Rewards, eh?"

"And one more thing..." Exodus stepped to the side and a woman popped into existence next to her. She had pitch-black skin with golden tattoos covering her body. Black feathered wings spread wide then folded in against her pristine white tunic.

"Oh, come on..." I grumbled.

"Query, this is—"

"Oh my, you're an Omegaian! Wait, hold on..." The woman brought out a book and quill from her leather pack. "Okay, can you tell me about your mating rituals?"

"Excuse me?" I said.

Exodus shook her head. "Actually, excuse her. This is Chronicle. She's...she will be keeping track of you on my behalf. I am breaching protocol just speaking with you. Anything you need, you go through her. I must go, but your mission starts now. Good luck, Query."

Then the child in rags ran off into the crowd and disappeared.

We sat in an awkward silence that eventually I needed to end. "So, you're a Valkyr?" I extended my hand to her. "The name's Query. Nice to meet you."

"Cool," she said, looking at my hand, then back at me. "I'll see you around. You can tell me about your mating rituals later."

She walked away leaving my hand extended to no one.

"Yeah, can't wait."

2

THE
EFFECTIVENESS
OF BRIBERY

Here's what I usually do to start tracking a bounty. I go to whatever dingy, snurl-infested grunkhole I've been staying at and drink myself into oblivion. Trust me, this part is essential.

Then I start by asking the big questions of the case like, what am I doing with my life? Why do I always do this to myself? Maybe I should have gotten into banking? There's also usually lots of crying. The next day, I'll begin tracking in earnest. Okay, here's where I actually start asking the big questions. Where and when was the individual last seen? Who saw them? What were they doing? And so on. The more information I gather, the more I learn about this person. The more I learn about them, the more I think like them, the easier I find them.

How easy will it be to find The Seeker?

Doesn't matter. Everyone slips, everyone gets caught.

Now that I think about it, usually I'm the one that does the seeking. Maybe whoever this is will make my job easier and come and find me first. If only it were that simple. Rule number something or other in bounty hunting is never underestimate the bounty. It doesn't matter if they're a fifty-foot giant or a two-foot-tall goblin. They have that bounty for a reason. If someone is turning dragons into ghosts, I probably don't want them finding me first. By being one, perhaps I too have something they want?

The dragons I "saw" in their ghost form were Extinct and Null—both of whom live on the planet Entropus. Currently, I'm on Separas, which is only two planets away. The good news is, I don't have to go around The Loop. Think of The Loop as the universe's biggest traffic jam of every conceivable being coming and going, all through the same space, all at the same time, pulsating with incredible magic, for all eternity. It's massive. The other good news is, unlike other creatures of the worlds, I don't have to rely on shuttles and ships to get me around Infinitus. I'm an interplanetary space dragon.

I can fly.

What can I say about flying in space? It can feel pretty intense. It's like flying inside a kaleidoscope of rainbows while riding a unicorn sharting cotton candy. After a while, it can feel like a Tuesday, but I still like to think I appreciate its beauty. I'd fly out the next morning. I just needed some sleep.

I was sitting in my snurl-infested grunkhole when there was a knock at my door.

Guess I'll sleep later.

I opened the door, and Chronicle stared back. "Yes?" I had had a few and was absolutely grunk-faced. I was lucky I was able to say that much.

"What's your plan?" Her quill and book were out before I noticed.

"Um...d'you wanna come in?" I leaned heavily against the door jamb. "There's a table...you can write on it maybe—"

"No."

"Oh...okay." She was really lucky getting this many words out of me. "So, you just wanna know the plan?"

"Yes. Tell me now please." Her glowing, pupil-less eyes bore holes into me.

I told her I was going to leave the next evening after I tied up some loose ends in Xeresis City, then I was flying directly to Entropus. She was to meet me back here tomorrow evening and we'd leave together. At least that's what I hope I said. It was probably more slurred growls than anything.

Regardless, she hummed to herself, wrote a final note in her book, and left me. Hopefully she was satisfied. I don't remember anything after that. Probably for the best.

I departed Separas the following morning sporting a horrific headache.

Damn, I gotta stop drinking so much...

Yes, I lied to Chronicle but this will be no surprise to anyone; I work alone. So, no Valkyr haunted my steps, for which I was thankful. Would it likely bite me in the tail later? I didn't care.

One unicorn with digestive issues later, I arrived on the planet Adjura. I would normally continue on to Entropus—having no desire to delay my mission—but there was someone that I wanted to visit first.

The planet Adjura is...weird. It wasn't a place where one could assume anything. So rather than buildings of steel and concrete like in Xeresis City, things were, well, alive. Things that would normally be inanimate are animals or plants. Street lights followed you as you walked underneath. Laughing bubbles bobbed in the breeze. Garbage cans gobbled up trash like gourmet meals. Ever been bitten by a door? I have. It's weird.

In the city of Brittanicus, lies the Library of Order. There are multiple layers of irony here that I can't let go. First, is that the Library of Order is led by the dragon, Order, but not named after the dragon, Order. Second, Order's method of order is not very orderly, at least not to the untrained eye, despite being called Order. It works for her, but for most people, it looks completely disorganized. What mattered was, she was incredibly knowledgeable and if anyone knew anything about what was going on with the ghosts and the dragons, it'd be her.

Before I visited her, I made the inevitable stop at a little store that sold sweets. This wasn't my first time visiting the dragon. The only thing that could take Order's mind off her insatiable obsession with knowledge was her insatiable appetite for candy. I didn't blame her, Adjura was known across Infinitus for its confections. And biting doors (I'm not over it yet).

I made it to the Library of Order just as the blue light of The Loop was setting in the western reaches. The Library was crafted out of the interweaving of tall, magnificent trees whose green and gold canopies sparkled up in the twilight. I caught myself before I grabbed the red furred door handle—that's how I got bit last time—and gave the door a few scratches with my talons. With a satisfied purr, it opened. The Library itself was a grand space filled with books, scrolls, papers, leaves with scribbled notes, and anything that could contain knowledge. It was a breathtaking sight to behold. Towering floor-to-ceiling shelves full of information. Order, on the other hand, was a tiny four-foot-tall dragon who looked more like a woodland creature than a magical being. Already inside I could hear her frantic scurrying. She fretted around as a brown and white blur, zipping to and fro on two legs in some unknowable mission to crack the code of the universe.

"Cohesion...cohesion has..." she muttered to herself, notes in hand.

"Hello?" I yelled into the cavernous library. "Order?"

"Cohesion has..."

"Order!"

"Hmm?" She still didn't look up from her notes. I knew what it would take, but sometimes it was nice to try the old fashioned way first. I reached into my pack, extracted a small leaf-woven pouch, and gave it a toss. It landed softly in my palm with a faint tinkling sound. Order abruptly stopped her infernal pacing. High into the air her nose went, twitching and smelling.

"Candies?" She smiled when she saw me. "Well, if it isn't my favorite, querical dragon."

It was that easy ladies and gentlemen. It was that easy.

"Querical isn't a word." I tossed her the pouch and her snout immediately dove into the bag. The sounds of crunching emanated throughout the library.

"It is; look it up."

She was probably right. "I have something to ask you."

"Yes, what can I do for you this time?"

I sat myself on the tiled floor not two paces away from her. It's hard talking down to a dragon like Order. Not only is it literally a massive pain in the neck to do so, but figuratively, she is far superior to me in her knowledge, and she deserves respect.

"Order, have you ever heard of someone called The Seeker?"

The crunching stopped. Her long, black and white ears flipped back, and she looked me dead in my eyes.

Jackpot!

"No. No...I have not!"

I threw my hands in the air. "Oh...well, why did you get all serious then?"

"Because I know a lot of things, and I know a lot of people, and yet I've never heard of The Seeker." She sidled up next to me. "Tell me everything you know."

"That's the thing..."

There wasn't much to tell as the mission just started, but I told her what I knew. I told her of Exodus and of the dragon ghosts I saw. She didn't touch a single candy as I spoke. That's how seriously she took the unknown. It only took a moment to tell her everything, but she asked questions, many questions.

Why are they called The Seeker?

I don't know.

Why are they going after dragons?

How should I know?

What do you think they smell like?

What does that have to do with anything?

This is what people talking to me must feel like. Nothing but questions. No wonder people roll their eyes when I show up.

"I will search the books for The Seeker, see if there is anything hidden in the tomes that might prove fruitful. You continue on to Entropus. Find out more. I'll help you all I can." She scooted away from me.

I stood up from the ground and stretched out my aching back. "Thanks, Order."

"You're very welcome." She leaned over and spoke behind me. "Chronicle, what do you think?"

"Wait, what?" I twisted around.

The Valkyr emerged from behind a bookshelf. Her leather bound book and golden quill already in hand. "I heard of The Seeker when they appeared on Entropus a few days ago. Null was the first dragon to engage with them. I was able to get some information, which I can give you."

"You what?" I was completely floored. "How did you get here...wait, what did you say? How come you didn't tell me this?"

"You didn't ask." There was no humor in her demeanor. She was completely serious.

"I thought we were supposed to be working together?"

"No." Chronicle corrected me. "I am only giving progress updates to the Ancients. This is your mission."

I turned back to Order and smiled. "I'll be back with more information. Thank you."

She didn't look up from her scrolls. "Yes, yes. I'll help. Bring more candies too!"

I turned between Chronicle with her book and Order with her library and sighed. "I will. Thanks."

Order resumed her frantic scurrying around the library, this time mumbling to herself about The Seeker. Had I known then what I know now, I never would have left her alone that night.

When Chronicle and I exited the Library of Order, it was fully dark. Lightbugs fluttered around with their glowing butts illuminating the streets. Chronicle was already a ways down the road before I noticed she'd left my side.

"Hey, wait." I jogged to catch up.

"Oh, hey Query!" she said without turning her gaze toward me.

"Yeah, hi...look. I kinda, well I thought you might be upset with me that I ditched you back on Separas." I attempted to gauge her emotional state. It was impossible yet again. "See the thing is—"

"I'm not mad."

"Oh, you're not?"

"No, why would I be mad?"

I continued to walk next to her for a few paces, trying to comprehend what was going on. "Um. Well, like I was saying I lied to you back on Separas, then you seemed upset because you were withholding information from me that might be, ya know, important, so...yeah that's about the long and short of it."

Her face didn't change. "Oh...but we aren't working together, so I figured you would do whatever you wanted and I would do whatever I wanted." She shrugged. "I didn't know you wanted to work together. Also, you didn't ask for information, so I didn't share any."

I nodded. "Yeah...yeah that makes sense. Should we work together then? What do you think?"

"No. I work alone."

"Yeah, I guess, so do I."

"Perfect."

I slowed my pace and let her walk away. "Yeah, perfect."

3

HOW'S THE HORNRAT?

The next day, and another psychedelic trip through space, I made it to Entropus. Alone.

Entropus was an insidious hellscape of fire and ice and it didn't care whether you lived or died. Okay, none of the planets cared whether you lived or died because they were nothing but giant rocks, but Entropus especially didn't care. Most of it was en flambé, meaning it was actively being destroyed by savage fires that burned so hot only the fiercest dragons dared tread. Other parts of Entropus were en icebé, which is actually a made-up word meaning it was a horribly frozen wasteland where nobody wanted to (or could) live. In between these awful, polar opposites were the lands of habitability. That's where everybody lived and warred with each other over small parcels of land that allowed for agriculture and overall sustainable living.

Yay war!

But Query, you're probably asking, *why don't they just get a shuttle and go somewhere else?* Oh, sure, of course it'd be that simple, except everything costs credits and when you're constantly at war and living off the land, you're poor, and being poor means you don't have any money. No money means no shuttles to paradise. Even if they could afford the shuttle, they needed money to survive and establish themselves on their new home world. One does not simply walk onto a new planet and live there. You needed money. See, it isn't that easy now, is it? Not everyone can have it as easy as an interplanetary space dragon like yours truly.

I landed in the middle of a desert jungle, one of the few I assumed that can survive the fires and the snows. It was chock full of thorns and colorful, deadly flowers. Nothing out of the ordinary. I double checked my list of ghost dragons. Using my magical scrying orb, I drifted off into the aether. To my horror, but unfortunately not my surprise, more of my dragon brethren had fallen into shells of themselves. In fact, the entire planet's dragons had fallen. Extinct, Null, Overhaul, and Chaos. *Grunk!*

Looking through the orb and sensing the position of the dragons, I was closest to Extinct, but that meant traversing the flame fields. Overhaul and Chaos were both acceptable, but also, pains in the ass. Fun fact about dragons, we don't get along with each other. Another fun fact, we actually fight with each other a lot. I don't get into that, just because I have better things to do, but that doesn't mean the others don't try to start fights with me. Whatever this ghost-ness meant, it hopefully knocked a bit of the fight out of them.

Hopefully.

That left Null. He was insufferable but not impossible. A giant worm of a dragon that had the ability of nullifying whatever magic or ability another dragon had. Hence the name. I know, we're good with names. It basically made him incredibly powerful. If The Seeker was able to take him down, I needed to know how. So Null it was.

Null lived by the cliffs of Sea'd, a coastal city in one of the few habitable zones of Entropus. Those that lived there were hard working, tough, and hearty people. They were protective of their livelihood and even more protective of their land. I respected them.

They didn't respect me back. Eh, no hard feelings. I'm a bounty hunter, respect isn't something that comes with the gig. That is, until I have binding cuffs on them. Then suddenly they all realize I'm the real deal.

I hiked most of the day before I hit the coast. Yes, I could have flown, but I wanted to enjoy the weather and stall as much as I could. It was nice smelling the fresh, clean air of open water and not being suffocated by the stifling cities of Separas or the bizarreness of Adjura. I followed the coast north to the town under the clear light of the blazing Loop above. Nothing interesting happened on the way there. I found a cool rock. Even thought about telling Chronicle about it. Maybe I'd give it to her. She could write about it. That'd keep her busy for a few hours.

It was too late to face Null, so I stopped at the tavern, named The Winged Scales, because let's be honest, traversing space then walking like a chump takes a lot of energy out of you and I was famished. The tavern was a ramshackle place, the kind that looked horrible on the outside with thick glass windows and a thatched roof, but made up for it with big helpings of delicious, greasy food. It was just what I needed.

The moment I walked in the door, everyone stopped talking and stared daggers at me. It wasn't that I was a dragon, it was because I was a stranger. As long as I minded my own business, paid my way, and left, there'd be no trouble. A tall, broad human woman, bronze skin with a mess of curly brown hair stood behind the bar polishing a dented tin cup. She had to be in her late twenties, maybe thirties, though her face looked like it felt the weight of more years than that. Around her neck was a ruby pendant hung on a gold chain. As I approached, a few of the patrons seemed to lose their thirst and moved away from the bar.

"You're scaring my customers, dragon."

Okay, it totally was because I was a dragon.

"Not my fault they're cowards." I probably could have been nicer about it, but whatever.

She sighed. "We don't serve your kind."

I reached into my pocket and tossed a few credits on the bar top. It was worth more than she'd see in a year. "Yes, you do."

"Yes," she replied with awe in her voice. "I surely do." She held a piece in the air and watched as the lantern light glinted off its metallic sheen. "What can I get you?"

"A hot meal and drink, if you have it."

She smiled. It seemed genuine. She pocketed the credits. "Of course I do. Only be a moment." She walked into a back room which I could only assume was the kitchen. After a second or two, she came back out and threw the towel she'd used to polish the cup over her shoulder. "So, you got a name?"

"Query."

"Folks call me Abby."

"Short for Abigail?"

"Yeah," she said as her gaze narrowed, "but the smart folks stick with Abby."

"Understood. Nice to meet you, I guess." I took one of the recently vacated seats at the bar. "Even though I had to bribe you to let me sit here."

"Oh," she said, waving a dismissive hand, "that's just all talk. Keeps the customers happy thinking I keep the riff raff out of here. I still would have taken care of you. It's what's fair."

"In that case I'll take my credits back."

Abby scoffed. "I still have to keep the business running."

"Alright...it's what's fair, as you say."

Abby grabbed a cup and filled it with a foul smelling liquid. "Here, this is what we drink. It puts hair on your chest and fire in your belly."

"Why would I want chest chair?"

"Just try it!"

Well, why not?

Did I mention I'm an interplanetary space dragon? A living marvel, wielder of the arcane, and overall supernatural being created by living ancient gods? I took a swallow and whatever was in this drink knocked me square on my ass. Hard. It felt like I had swallowed an ice cube that was on fire but the ice cube was made of fire and the fire was frozen. Spicy ice—that's how I would describe it. Spicy ice multiplied by a million.

The entire tavern howled watching me suffer through that terrible drink. Even Abby, who at first was trying to keep it together, was laughing so hard she started a coughing fit, one that racked her body. She brought her towel up to her mouth and it came back splattered red.

"Are you okay?" I asked, still wheezing from the drink.

"Yeah, yeah. Just a lingering cough I can't seem to shake. How'd ya like our drink? I call it Spicy Ice."

I pushed the cup away, admittedly frightened I'd be made to take another swig. "I couldn't agree more with that name. It's something I'll have to get used to, I guess."

She cocked an eyebrow. "Are you planning on sticking around, then?"

"Maybe. Depends on how the first day goes."

Abby looked like she wanted to ask more, but just then a bell rang from the back. She went to the back room and returned with an entire roasted hornrat, golden and still sizzling on a wooden platter. This one was the size of my head. Roasted tubers lined the sides and half a loaf of fresh baked bread was served on a smaller plate. Dragons are primarily carnivores, but the aroma of the veggies and bread made me reconsider.

"This looks amazing. Thank you, Abby."

"The finest your money can buy." She smiled. "Tim?" She yelled to a human male sitting at a booth in the rear of the tavern. "You mind helping me out and chopping some more wood for the fireplace? I haven't had a chance to get to it."

"Sure!" Tim, a peasanty looking fellow, popped up and ran out the door like a child trying to impress his parents. Soon the sounds of axe blows and split wood could be heard outside.

I swallowed a mouthful of hornrat. "He work for you?"

"No. I'm lucky I guess, people like to do things for me. Probably because I do things for them."

"Like what?"

"Most of the time, people come to me with their problems and I listen. Most of the time, I come up with solutions that people like. Sometimes, if there are fights between people, I help them figure it out."

"Like a judge?"

"I guess so."

"Interesting."

"What do you do, Query?"

I swallowed another bite of succulent hornrat leg. "Like my name says. I ask questions."

"Oh? What kind of questions do you ask?"

"Just general ones. For example, where does someone with a bartender's income, who gets excited over a few silvery credits, get a pretty pendant like that?" Abby instinctively reached for the trinket around her neck, protecting it for whatever was to come. "Now before you get offended, I'm not saying you stole it, not at all. In fact. I think you are the type of person who has perhaps lowered herself to this position from something far higher. Am I getting close?"

She stroked her pendant like it was the most precious thing in her world. I waved a dismissive, grease-covered hand. "Never mind. That's far too personal for having just met. Let's try another one. Have you ever heard of The Seeker?"

Abby's eyes went wide. Her lower lip trembled as a near imperceptible tremor graced her mouth. "No," she whispered, "can't say I have."

4

SOMEWHERE
OVER THE
RAINBOW

Questions are like keys. Keys open locks. Each lock that is opened reveals a greater truth, regardless of the answer. Abby's truth was that she knew much more than she was saying. This is why I always watch when getting an answer. Had I not, I would have missed all her body language telling me she had, in fact, heard of The Seeker. Here is all the information it gives us. The Seeker has been to Entropus—we knew that because of the ghost dragons—but now we know that they've also visited the people of Sea'd. Why? What do people have to do with their grand plan? Another question to answer. Maybe Abby was covering for them? Or maybe she was terrified? My gut says terrified. I've been around people. I know the difference between being scared for your life and being scared you'll get found out. So why would The Seeker attack dragons *and* hassle the locals?

I finished my meal in silence, said my goodbye, and left Abby to her duties. The air outside was brisk and the wind off the ocean smelled of brine. To my left, Tim happily hacked away at a growing pile of logs. I thought nothing of him at first, but then, something nagged at the back of my mind.

"Hey, Tim?"

The man jumped nearly four feet in the air. He turned and held the axe high over his head. "D-d-d-don't eat me d-d-d-dragon!"

"Eat you?" I let out a laugh, which now in retrospect may or may not have sounded like a hideous growl. "Did you not see me in there eating the hornrat? I don't eat humans, idiot." Tried it once, no flavor.

Be cool, Query, he's only a dumb human.

"Um, sorry. ...why are you chopping wood for Abby?"

Tim still held the axe up high, ready to swing. "I uh...I don't know. She asked me to, I guess."

"Are you normally just a nice guy?"

Tim's mouth fell open. My question seemed to throw him off and he lowered the axe. "Uh...my mother thinks so."

"Very truthful of you, Tim." I walked up to him. "So, if I understand, you just feel compelled to help Abby?"

"Y-y-y-yeah. That's a good word for it. Compelled."

"Hmm..." I paused, trying to think of anything else to say. Nothing came. I slapped Tim on the back. "Whelp, back at it, Champ!" I turned and left him to his chopping.

That night I found my dingy, snurl infested, grunk-hole east of town. Home sweet home I call it. It actually was quite nice. I shouldn't complain. The room was decently furnished at least.

It was late and I was tired. Alright, let's get another personal question out of the way. I'm embarrassed that you're even thinking it, but I'll answer it anyway. How do dragons sleep? Just like every other creature. Why would we be any different? Seriously, maybe take some time and reflect upon yourself for a while. Okay fine, dragons don't like beds. Our scales and spikes usually tear them to shreds. The floor is totally fine. Happy?

The next morning I awoke to pristine brilliant light from The Loop sparkling over the open sea. It was as if the day was taunting me into believing it wouldn't be an absolute chore. I knew it would be, so I took the long road out to see good old Null.

I've mentioned before that we dragons don't get along. It doesn't mean we don't care for each other, but think of it like sibling rivalry. There is a bit of pleasure seeing each other miserable, but deep down inside some of us still care. I do at least...sometimes.

I had the suspicion he hadn't moved since his encounter with The Seeker. The ground was turned up and rutted. Null was twisted up into a tight coil, with his gigantic spikes protruding out in all directions, his head buried deep inside. It was a posture of defense. I'd never once seen a dragon–let alone a beast like Null–behave like this. A chill ran down my spine, and it wasn't from the wind. I could tell by the rise and fall of his body that he was still alive. I called out to him, being as sensitive as possible. "Null, you big baby, open up!"

Nothing.

"Null, talk to me!"

Nothing. Nothing but nothing. Which was weird when I realized I felt nothing. Normally, when hanging around Null, there was always this inexplicable feeling of loss. I mentioned I'm an interplanetary space dragon, right? I feel like I have. I must have. Anyway, I use magic and when I'm around Null, that magic is gone. Can't use it. However, today, I could still feel it coursing through me. Null was no longer nulling.

I walked up to the great dragon—great in size, not in personality—and slammed my fist against his armored plates. "Come on you big dumb bastard! Open up! I'm trying to help you!"

Slowly, his plates grated against themselves as his defensive coil loosened, revealing a gap between his body. From the darkness within, two piercing ice-blue eyes peered out at me.

"Query," he hissed. "Are you alone?"

I scoffed. "You know I am."

"Why are you here?"

"Exodus, if you believe it, sent me. I'm after The Seeker."

Null nervously looked around as if mentioning the name would summon the entity.

"You're either brave, or foolish to go after it." An evil cackle came from within the depths of its self-imposed prison. "I know you aren't brave so you must be the fool."

"Dammit, I'm here to help, cut the crap and let me ask my questions."

"Fine." Its body rose and fell in a sigh. "Ask."

Seriously, dragons, what a pain in the ass. "Let's start off easy, what'd they look like?"

"Garbed in a black, hooded robe, its body was of black smoke."

I impatiently scratched at one of my head spikes. "So it isn't a person I'm looking for, but some sort of ethereal being? Super. An amazing detail that Exodus left out. What else, anything else significant about their appearance?"

The serpent nodded its head and then added, "it was a Glyph."

"A Glyph?"

"Yes, this it confirmed, but what Glyph I do not know. I do know what it did."

"And that was?"

"It severed my link to the aether."

That's it. That's why I still felt my magic. So it was The Seeker's Glyph that took Null's abilities. I bet that they had taken Extinct's, Overhaul's, and Chaos's abilities too. But why are they just ghosts in my scrying orb? There was a reason, but it was secondary. Finding The Seeker was my only priority.

"Last question: any idea why they would visit the city? Visit people?"

"No," the dragon quickly replied.

"Great. Thanks." Null, the most helpful dragon in Infinitus.

"Now leave me," he said, "you've kept me vulnerable for far too long!" His coils tightened and his head and ice-blue eyes disappeared.

Null would tell me nothing else of use, so I left him alone in his self-made battlement.

"Did you learn anything new?" A voice said behind me.

I almost grunked my pants. The Valkyr stared at me, as always quill and book at the ready.

"Chronicle!" I grabbed at my chest. "You can't sneak up on people like that. I could've hurt you!"

"I don't think so. What did you learn from Null?"

I ground my teeth. "Why don't you ask him yourself?" I started walking down the road.

"But, I asked you," she yelled back.

I decided I didn't hear her.

By evening I was back in Sea'd.

I sat in my room and thought about my information. I now had a description and a modus operandi of The Seeker. Next, I needed a motive. That was an easy one. Stealing dragon abilities can make you very powerful. So prestige, tyrannical, maniacal ideation...seems pretty cut and dry. Classic bad guy stuff. I can't assume that's the *only* motive, but for now, it seems like the best bet. Description, operations, motives, and lastly, pattern. I needed to know where they are going to strike next. This was going to be near impossible. Was The Seeker simply collecting dragon abilities? Was there a specific order they were going in? Going planet to planet?

Travel... okay, this is an area I can look into right now. I don't think I've mentioned it, but I'm an interplanetary space dragon. I can fly through space. Everyone else needs ships and shuttles and other banal methods of travel. Unless The Seeker was a shape-shifter, I doubt an ethereal being would be taking the 9:45 to Separas. I closed my eyes, brought up my pink orb, and sifted through dragons. Those of Entropus were in their shell form, but looking through some of the other planets, I noticed there was one dragon that was noticeably...noticeable.

Peek. That sneaky little...

Peek is a dragon that can disappear and reappear two feet away, or two miles away, or—if his power is at maximum—an entire planet away utilizing wormholes. I looked to Adjura and Antaia. Both planets had their dragons bright and full. Guessing which direction The Seeker would go was as good as a coin flip. I could wait for another dragon to become a ghost of themselves. At least that would give me the planet, but that seemed reckless. And a jerk thing to do. I'll have to think about it.

I opened my eyes and the black pits of Infernus stared back at me.

5

RUDE
AWAKENINGS

Sickly lips curled, revealing a mouthful of dark fangs. Her thin, pale skin failed to hide the black veins that crossed her face below. A shock of wild, tasseled coal-black hair grew from her head. Black obsidian eyes, weeping blood, stared back at me. I only saw the face for a moment. The next, her hands were at my throat squeezing. Her power was incredible, but I'm an interplanetary space dragon, and I'm no slouch in a fight. My claws flung out like razorblades and slashed at her sides, I flashed my teeth and gnashed at her face.

She wasn't even phased.

Desperately, I grabbed onto both of her arms and yanked. Nothing. My vision began to blur as my brain lacked its much needed oxygen. In a final push, I kicked out violently, sending her across the room. She got up on all fours, growling at me. I was on my feet, rubbing life back into my neck. Fine, I was a slouch in an infernal spawn fight. Who knew? I'd never seen anything like this creature before. I called her that only because that's the closest thing I could think of. She launched herself at me again. I spun and dodged, but she had claws of her own and raked them across my face. I howled in pain. I saw my chance with her back turned, I balled my fist and struck her where previously I had slashed her. My hand came back covered in a thick, red ichor.

Damage.

So she could bleed?

She struck at me again and I grabbed her wrist. She struck at me with the other hand and I caught that wrist too. I held both arms in check and thought I had the advantage until she made to sink her dark fangs into my hand. I don't like getting bit. I really don't like getting bit. I released her wrist, while still holding the other. Quickly I struck her head as hard as I could, then again, and again, and again. That fourth strike seemed to be enough to do her in.

I stood, breath heaving my chest, as the creature lay unconscious at my feet. I'd love to say this was the first time someone has tried to kill me. It wasn't. First time I've fought a spawn of Infernus? Yep, this is a new one. However, this might be good news. I might be sticking my snout where it doesn't belong and upsetting someone. I'm on the right track. That or the town has a *huge* monster infestation. In that case, I'm outta here!

I checked over the woman or creature or whatever she was. She seemed like a she. She wore dark rags, like a beggar. Upon her forehead was emblazoned a fierce red marking of which its meaning I could not tell. I got out my binding cuffs just to be safe and I clamped her hands behind her back. Yes, of course the binding cuffs are magic. She's going to have a tough time getting out of those. Now, what was I supposed to do with her? I can't just dump her outside. I doubt the local constabulary would know what to do with her either.

"What am I supposed to do with you?" I asked her, as if she would answer.

She didn't, thankfully.

I did the only thing I could think of. I sat down on the floor and watched her. I watched her for hours, trying to think of anything, something I could use against her. The only thing I got was more tired. I'm a pretty good bounty hunter. In fact, I'm probably the best, but a watchman...watchdragon, I am not. The next thing I knew, the whimpers of a woman were waking me from slumber. Panicked, I searched for the monster, but she was gone. Instead a new surprise awaited me.

Sitting where the creature sat the night before, trapped in my own binding cuffs, was Abby, the tavern bartender.

"Hey," she said, her awkward smile betrayed her embarrassment.

I cocked a weary eye at her. "Hey..."

"Um...do you mind letting me out?"

"You're going to stay right there crazy lady. Not until I figure this out." There was no way I was going to figure this out. "Okay, do you know what's going on?"

Abby wouldn't look me in the eyes. Her curly hair fell over her face. "Yes...and no."

I paced the small room. "Alright. Let's start with what you know."

She tipped her head back and blew a lock of hair out of her face which sparked a coughing fit. I rushed to the bedside table and grabbed a cup of water. I handed it to her, then remembering her hands were still bound behind her back, I berated myself and held it up to her mouth. She drank greedily. A few more coughs and she composed herself. "I promise that it's over for now."

"For now?"

"She only comes out at night, I think. I don't know for sure."

I looked her over again. I wasn't sure what to believe.

"I'm starving; she takes most of my energy. I need food."

I glared at her. "This isn't some trick, is it? I let you go, you change back into that *thing* and devour my soul or something wacky like that?"

"I don't think it's that simple."

I looked out the window. Dark clouds hung in the sky and rain threatened to spoil the day. I took the blanket from the bed, pulled Abby up to standing, and wrapped the blanket around her like a cloak. "Just stay like this. Let me think about it."

We exited the grunk-hole just as a light drizzle began and walked down the mud caked streets of Sea'd. Like all cities of Infinitus, Sea'd was a cavalcade of creatures that shared more in culture than in species. It was a truly beautiful thing if you're into that. Most people don't give two spoons of snurl slime. A Dosnian doesn't care if a Homina or a Komaplo moves in next door as long as they respect the local culture. Now say a Freebnar comes in but celebrates Westerfest but abhors Yood? Now you've got trouble. Let me tell you something, you don't want to be anywhere near a Freebnar fight during Westerfest. Jornplum juice everywhere. The point is, a dragon and a cloaked human weren't a terribly weird combination. We still drew the odd look here and there. Also it seemed no one could tell, or cared she wore binding cuffs.

We reached The Winged Scales just as thunder cracked and the sky opened up its water. You'll never guess who was outside. Tim. That's right, Tim was still hacking at the fire wood. Poor guy.

"Ah, Tim!" Abby ran to him. The blanket came tumbling off. Luckily I had the wherewithal to snap the cuffs off quickly so no one could see them. Plus, if she decided to turn back into a monster, hopefully she'd eat Tim first.

"Tim, it's okay, you can stop now. Go home and rest."

"Uhhhhhh," he said. He dropped the axe. "Why did I chop so much?" He shambled off home like a walking corpse.

Abby turned back to me. "I forgot, I have to tell them when to stop too, otherwise people just keep working."

"That's weird. Do you know why?"

"I have no clue. Just always happens that way." She rubbed her wrists where the binding cuffs had been. "Thanks for taking the cuffs off. They were really digging."

"Yeah, no problem." I didn't tell her about eating Tim. "They're binding cuffs. They don't just physically bind you, they also bind your essence. Even magic couldn't get you out of those."

She smiled. "Well, thank you anyway. Come on, let's get me that food. You're buying. Then, I'll tell you everything I know. You won't even have to ask me any questions." She walked through the tavern door, leaving me alone in the street.

"But I like asking questions."

6

WORK SUCKS,
I KNOW

It was just like all the other days in Sea'd for Abby. The perpetual clouds from Entropus's mixture of extreme heat and extreme cold enveloped the town, bringing on a depression the denizens rarely shed, even on the rare days the Looplight shone through.

She'd grown up in the city, but wasn't born there. In fact, she didn't know where she was born. Her parents had emigrated to Entropus from Deltaria when they couldn't survive its ultra-capitalistic society, but whether she was with them then, or before then, she didn't know. They'd died when she was young.

Too young.

Remembering their faces was like waking up from a dream and you can't place the details, but you understand the meaning. Emotions. That was the better word for it. That's what she felt toward her parents. Not visuals, sounds, or even scents. She felt emotions. Love, kindness, but also ferocity. They had fought for her, cared for her. Since their deaths, she'd done that all by herself.

Now, all she did by herself was serve breakfast, lunch, dinner, and last call. That night it was just her in the tavern; everyone had gone home. The tables were wiped, the stools up on the table tops, and the fire in the hearth was nothing but smoldering orange embers. It was finally time to go.

"Demura ek shaa grep tha..."

Abby spun, looking for whoever whispered in her ear. Her mop held like a spear, ready to strike. This wasn't the first time someone thought to take advantage of the lone female bartender late at night.

There was nothing.

Outside the wind howled like tortured specters.

Of course, it was the wind.

There were more drafts in the walls of the old building than they had on tap. It was the wind and nothing more.

The unintelligible words whispered in both ears this time, one voice high, the other low.

"Demura ek shaa grep tha..."

"Yup, I'm outta here!" Abby threw the mop on the floor and walked out of the tavern. She didn't bother locking up. The thieves could take whatever money was left in the till, she didn't care, it wasn't much anyway. Outside was dark, darker than normal. The moons of Entropus shed no light that evening. The streets were devoid of people, as if the entire town were in slumber. Despite the late hour, she'd usually see a local constable or late night partiers out and about. But tonight the streets were empty, black, and foreboding.

A chill ran through her, not because of temperature, but because she felt a presence with her, one she couldn't see. She turned and walked toward home.

"Demura ek shaa grep tha!" A chorus sang, a thousand voices rang out as one in a deafening roar. Abby fell to her knees—a heavy weight bore down on her. Before her, barely visible against the dark backdrop of night, a figure stood, arms raised, as if in adoration of some obscene god.

"Demura ek shaa grep tha!" it called again. "I am The Seeker. Join your voice with mine. Together we will sing the lament of Infinitus and prepare for the coming of Paracyst!"

Abby fought to move, but her body was bound by an invisible force. She attempted to scream, but her voice was cut off, the force constricted her with every breath, like a serpent and its prey. The Seeker came forward, floating on black mist. Abby squirmed but was held fast. It came closer, it drew her in, pressed her against itself in a fell embrace. She felt its nothingness. The Seeker bent low and whispered in her ear. "Do not fight it, child of abomination. I am making you what you were meant to become."

There was a sharp pain in her neck, a bite, and something flowed from The Seeker into her. Inside she felt a force growing, pulsating, breathing as if it were alive. She looked down, her skin rumbled, as if it hid something, a living thing, like a hideous alien. It ran itself over and through her. It enveloped her body and consumed her. The last thing she heard was the chorus chanting its evil song.

"Demura ek shaa grep tha...Demura ek shaa grep tha..."

Abby woke up in her own bed, in her own house, on her own street. The morning light lay dappled around her. She sat up and quickly checked her neck, making sure there were no teeth marks. Nothing. No marks, bumps, indents, or holes. Nothing that would have indicated she was attacked by a cloaked smoke monster. Abby went to her wash basin and splashed water on her face. In the mirror, she looked like her normal self, maybe a bit darker around her eyes. It was a dream, it had to be a dream. A nightmare. She'd been working too much. That had to be the issue. She got to work when it was still dark in the mornings and left when it was dark in the evenings. Of course she'd dream of darkness consuming her.

It only made too much sense.

That's when she coughed.

Not a little tickle in her throat, but a hard, hacking cough. She coughed and coughed, it racked her body with pain until finally, one last hack and something flew from her mouth and into the basin. She gasped when she saw blood. Blood, mixed with a bit of black ooze.

I cleaned the flue to the hearth yesterday morning before I started a fire...it's only soot. I'll just wear a wet cloth around my mouth next time.

Abby went to work, like it was any other day.

She served breakfast, lunch, dinner, and last call.

Once again, it was night and she found herself alone in the tavern. Cleaning up after people who were old enough to know how to clean up after themselves. It was a thankless job, but a job was a job and she was lucky enough to have it. Every creak of the floor, every gust of the wind, even seeing her reflection in the glass windows caused her to startle. In fact, after a while something with her reflection felt wrong. The light in the tavern was dim, only a few lanterns burned, but it was obvious to her that her hair, normally a chestnut brown, was midnight black. She pulled at it and looked with her eyes, and in the lantern light, it seemed its normal hue. She looked back in the reflection and her hair again appeared like pitch. Her eyes had changed as well. The eyes that stared back at her were two oil drops, black and cruel. She squeezed them shut and looked again, and yet they persisted as two empty voids. She frantically covered them with her hands.

What's happening to me? Am I going insane?

She pulled her hands away. They were covered with blood and her skin had turned pale, translucent, allowing her dark veins to be seen. It felt tight, thin, as if it would burst off of her. Her nails grew into dark, sharp claws. She looked back at her reflection and she didn't recognize the person she saw. It was no longer her.

"Greetings, child of abomination," came the voices of the chorus.

Abby, the monster, turned, flitted her head back and forth, searching. She found the figure standing inside the tavern. Her eyesight became tunneled, acute. She only saw the cloaked figure. She felt her body move in compliance to a force she could not perceive, but knew was there. She knew this figure and knew it was righteous. She bowed to it in submission.

Without thinking, she said "I join my voice to yours, I shall sing the lament of Infinitus and its people. I shall obey you, the herald and bringer of Paracyst!"

"Good. Now rise. Rise, my child. Rise, my Demura. Rise...my Tyranny! Destroy those who stand in our way! Destroy! Destroy!"

"Yes, Master. I will...*destroy!*"

7

I TAKE ATTEMPTED MURDER PERSONALLY

I nodded and set down my cup. The Spicy Ice didn't hit me as hard as it had the day before. In fact, I was starting to understand the subtle nuances of its harsh flavor. I was also starting to understand that Abby wasn't a crazy monster lady after all, but a victim. A victim of The Seeker, if I was to believe her. At this point, I had no reason not to.

"Do you know who or what this Paracyst thing, person, is?"

Abby shook her head, her curls bouncing over her shoulders, her eyes never left her untouched cup. "I don't know."

I shrugged. At the moment, this Paracyst wasn't the main issue. I'd tell Chronicle about it—whenever she decided to show up again—and let her deal with it. I was after the guy that turned dragons into ghosts, enthralled the town's barkeeper, and turned her into something called a Demura. A Demura that tried to kill me. I take attempted murder personally.

"Why you?"

Abby looked up from her drink. "What?"

"Why you? Of all the people here in town, why choose you? No offense, but why are you so special?"

She gave a half-hearted smile and played with the ruby pendant around her neck. "I-I don't know. As far as I know, I am just like every other human out here. Just trying to make a living. Serving drinks, helping people where I can."

There was one thing about her that did stick out that I hadn't given much thought to until now. "Have you noticed that you are almost a full head taller than most of the humans around here?"

She scrunched her eyebrows and shrugged. "I'm tall, so what? What does that have to do with anything?"

"And that pendant of yours, the thing you keep touching...seems to be magical. What does it do?"

Her gaze drifted out the dirty windows. "I don't want to talk about it."

She remained silent as I finished my food. "This is a big problem for me, see, it's my job to bring in or take down The Seeker, and it seems it's your job to stop me from doing that. So what do we do?"

"But I don't want to stop you." Abby pushed her food away and leaned in. "I want to help you."

"Then what are you hiding from me? What aren't you telling me?"

She said nothing.

I held out my hands. "See? How is this going to work if you don't work *with* me?"

Her eyes drilled holes into me. "That's it! I'm working with you. It's decided. You're stuck with me now. We're doing this together."

"Whoa, that's not what I meant. I work alone."

"What's the alternative? You go off on your own while I stay a Demura forever? I want to be done with this curse too!"

"And we have a fight every night until either I knock you out and lock you up, or you kill me? No way! One of us is going to die before this is all over."

Abby looked me dead in the eyes. "We're working together."

"Exactly, we're working together! And that's final!" I growled, standing up, nearly knocking our table over.

Wait, what just happened? I think she just Timmed me. Grunk, I've been Timmed! I don't understand, one moment I am vehemently against everything she is saying and in the next moment, it all makes beautiful, perfect sense. Of course she needs to come with me. Together we can figure out what's going on with The Seeker, and hopefully help her along the way. It's brilliant. I wish I had thought of it.

No, I didn't. Bah!

She settled her affairs with the tavern keeper, who was sad to see her go, but at this point I was so antsy to get moving that I didn't have time to care for emotions. We stopped by Abby's place so she could change, pack a knapsack and some other things she thought were necessary. One of the items was wrapped in an oilcloth.

"What's that?" I already knew what it was, but sometimes playing dumb is better than being a know-it-all.

She undid the cloth and revealed a dagger. A brilliant piece of weaponry with gems embedded in its golden hilt and an edge so keen it looked like it had never been used.

"Where did you get such a thing?"

"Ah, this? Just a family heirloom. Nothing more. I wouldn't know the first thing about how to use it. Come on, let's get going."

I was still planning on visiting with Extinct, but now that I had a horribly mortal human hanging out with me, I didn't want to risk hurting her. In case you were wondering, yes, we interplanetary space dragons are mortal as well, but there is a big difference between dragon mortal, and human mortal. Comparatively in order for a dragon to be killed, they would need to be choked, stabbed, bludgeoned, maimed, and quartered. A human would need a stiff breeze and slight humiliation. It's night and day. So yes, I was effectively babysitting.

Super.

"Where to?" Abby asked as we left down the road leaving town. "I assume you have a grand plan?"

"Yes," I lied. "There is only one logical place that The Seeker is going to strike next."

"Where is that?"

I stopped and took a final look out over the waters and inhaled the saltiness of the ocean. I was stalling, not because I really didn't know where to go next, but because when I retired, if I retired, I realized it would be in a place like this. Not the bustling cities, but a calm coastal town. I could get along with these people.

I think. Yeah...probably. Why not?

"Query? Hello?"

"Yeah, I know." I turned back around to look at Abby. "Like I said, there is only one place The Seeker would show up." I walked past Abby. There, standing in the middle of the road, was a black visage, wreathed in smoke.

"Abby?"

"Yeah?"

"That them?"

She saw me looking past her and turned. "Yeah."

"Thought so." I took a few steps closer. "Took you long enough!"

"Query, what are you doing?" Abby whispered.

"When I realized last night that one of the dragons that Seekster here ghosted was Peek, only a fully powered Peek could move off planet, and with The Seeker zipping around the planet doing their thing, they'd have to wait awhile to regain full power. Therefore, when they found out I was hot on their trail, they sent their Demura after me. When that didn't work, they decided to take care of me themselves. Isn't that right?"

The Seeker remained still and rather unenthused with my speech, so I decided to be stupid about it.

I approached The Seeker. "I have a wager for you, if you'll take it." I reached into my pocket and took out my deck of cards. Before I could finish my offer, the deck exploded in my hands and rained down as wispy ashes.

Extinct. I could smell her destructive brimstone.

The Seeker raised their arms much as Abby had described the night it turned her into the spawn of Infernus creature. The last thing I needed was for her to get caught up with them again and the only thought that came to mind was to protect her. Without thinking it through, I rushed The Seeker. As I reached out with my claws, it vanished and reappeared at my side. I pivoted, swung hard again only to swipe at nothingness. I growled and spun again, and again, and again. Nothing but air. Frustrated, I ditched the idea of hurting them, and just wanted them to stop teleporting. In a stroke of luck (it sure wasn't skill) I got a hold of their dark vestments. On instinct, I reached into my pocket and out came my magical binding cuffs. I slapped them around one of their wrists.

"Gotcha," I yelled triumphantly. The Seeker only laughed and the cuff promptly fell right off.

Null. I could feel his magic pacification.

Now I'm terrified.

The Seeker opened their cloak and there, suspended in a field of smoke was the gemstone. Black as night, yet shined with every color imaginable. It was breathtaking. I couldn't take my eyes off it. Behind me, Abby was yelling something, but I couldn't hear her. The gem. It was calling to me. A million voices called, inviting me to live with it forever. I wanted to. I needed to.

Then came the pain.

Searing pain within my soul. I fell to the ground and writhed as if my insides were being torn out of me. My screams echoed over the waters and were lost over the endless seas of Entropus. My body tensed and twitched as the pain coursed through my body. Abby watched on helplessly. I dug my claws into the dirt and braced myself against the endless torture inflicted upon me. The Seeker looked down upon me as I gasped for breath and the chorus gave me one final threat. "Join our song, or your order will be purged." Then they were gone and the pain fled me.

I woke up as if from sleep. Groggy and confused, I hefted myself off the ground and staggered to Abby. My world spun in chaos. Her voice was muffled. She was saying something, but I couldn't understand.

"Query!"

I understood that.

Oh...oh no...did he?

I staggered past her and collapsed on the ground again. I sat, shut my eyes, and tried to concentrate. Nothing. I tried harder. Again, nothing. Try as I might, nothing was happening. I had no idea he was that powerful. No, I did know, I was just too arrogant. I should have been more cautious. He severed my link to the aether, just like the others. Helpless, I started to weep.

Abby came and knelt down beside me. "Query, what? What happened?"

"I can't see them anymore..."

"Who? Who can't you see?"

"Dragons," I said as I looked into her eyes, tears welling in mine. "I can't see the dragons anymore, and now that bastard can!"

8

ADJURA OR
ANTAIA

I don't know how long I sat there. In the face of loss, time can lose all meaning. For a while, Abby just sat and held me. I didn't ask for it, but I didn't ask her to stop. How could I be so arrogant? How could I be so naive to think a dragon like me could simply capture an ethereal being like that? I'm only an interplanetary space dragon, what could I do against such power?

"Query?" Abby gently shook my shoulders, an attempt to snap me out of it. "Query, we need to go."

"Yeah...okay," I can only feel sorry for myself for so long. I still needed much more time to feel sorry, but evidently Abby didn't. "We need to go, but I don't know where."

Abby pulled me in front of her and did that thing where she looked deep into my eyes. "Come on, you're smart. Think. Where could they be going? You said they could only teleport to a neighboring planet. Adjura or Antaia. Which one?"

I shook my head. "I don't know...I—"

Voices. There were so many voices inside The Seeker. Some whispered to me, others spoke, while others screamed. Yet, through their hideous din, something The Seeker had said crept through. But could it be that simple? Did they tell me where they were going without realizing it, or were they goading me now that I am impotent in my powers? Yes, it only made too much sense. By the Ancients...we needed to move.

"What is it?" Abby asked.

"I know where they are going." I picked myself off the ground. "Abby, do you trust me?"

There was a look on her face as if she'd known me all her life, instead of the two days since we'd met. I don't know why this was, or why I knew the answer before she spoke. I unfurled my wings, wrapped them around her, and held her tight. "Have you ever been to space?"

"When I was a little girl, but I don't remember much of it."

"You'll remember this."

The ground around us trembled. Pebbles rose off the ground and floated in mid air. A moment of pure silence, then we launched into the air like a screaming rocket, billowing rainbow exhaust behind us. The Seeker may have taken our specific abilities, but not the magic that made us dragons.

I, often, if not constantly, take for granted what it's like to be a dragon. Remember what I said it was like to fly through space? *Like flying inside a kaleidoscope of rainbows while riding a unicorn sharting cotton candy.* Abby was experiencing that for the first time (don't worry, she'll survive; it's magic after all). I got to live that again through her and watching her, awestruck, made me feel like a little dragon again, all those thousands of years ago. I have lived such a long life, and Abby's has been just a blink of an eye. Amazing what I would have missed had I not stopped to befriend a human.

We're friends now? Yeah, I kinda guess we are. I never would have imagined it. This must be what it's like to have a child, looking at the world through new eyes. Seeing everything through a new lens. I'm gonna have to get used to this, but I think I'm going to like it.

"Hey, Query?"

"Yeah?"

"I have to pee."

Damn humans. I'm not gonna like this. Not one bit.

Your order will be purged...

At face value, it was a threat meant to drag me into the depths of futility. The Seeker was going to destroy all of the dragons. Anyone who was anyone would have understood it to mean that, but it's also kind of a weird way of putting it because no one has ever referred to dragons as an order. It's when Abby returned some confidence to me that I understood what The Seeker meant. It wasn't a threat, they were goading me. They were saying "you want to try again, here's where to find me."

They were going to Adjura, the home of the dragons Coax, Fierce, Purge...and I know which one they were visiting first.

Order. They're going to take Order's knowledge, and not only do they know exactly where to find her, they teleported to Adjura while I have to take the long way and fly there.

Damn Query...Damn arrogant Query!

We landed in Adjura, just outside the Library of Order. It looked nothing like it did the other day. The door was ripped off its hinges and lay whimpering off to the side. Papers, books, and many other things were strewn about outside, like an explosion had occurred inside the Library. I went up to the door and gently pet it. "Shh...it's okay buddy. We're gonna take care of the guy that did this to you, don't worry." The door purred back and seemed satisfied with my promise.

Abby came up and rubbed her hand over the door. "Friend of yours?"

I was focused on what awaited us inside. "Something like that. Come on, let's go in."

We entered the Library of Order. Everything was a mess. Sitting on the floor, the diminutive dragon sniffled and shuffled through sheets of papers and countless scrolls. I could smell the brimstone of The Seeker here. I knelt down to get eye-level with her. "Order, are you okay?"

"Candies, for Order?" she said.

"Uh, sorry, no candies." I patted my pockets. "I promise to get you some before I leave. Tell me everything that happened here."

She wiped a tear from her eye. "Order doesn't know. Order doesn't know anything. No more books in Order's head. No more knowledge. Query...I know nothing."

I understand taking the abilities of most of us dragons. A lot of us can be absolute assholes. But not her. She is the sweetest, kindest dragon you'll ever meet. There isn't a sour bone in her body. I rubbed her shoulders and gave her the same promise I gave Bitey Door. That's right, I named the door. Do what you want to Null and the others; they are overgrown, self-absorbed babies. But don't you dare do anything to Order. I take that personally.

"Order, The Seeker got me too." I pointed over my shoulder to Abby. "We're going to take him down. I promise you that."

"Candies, for Order?"

I smiled at the now dumb little dragon. "Yes, I'll get you candies. Abby, can you watch her? I need to run an errand. I'll be right back."

"Sure thing. I got her."

I left the Library of Order to get its keeper some candies.

9

OUT OF ORDER

A bby sat down next to the weeping Order. Everywhere surrounding her was devastation. She marveled at it all, and thought about what it once was, or what it could have been had she seen it before its destruction. Her daydream was short as the weeping dragon grabbed her attention.

"Hi, I'm Abby. It's nice to meet you."

The dragon looked up from her wallowing and seemed to see Abby for the first time. "Hello, Abby."

"Say, do you remember what you were researching before the being in black arrived?"

Order shook her head.

Abby rethought the question and tried again. "How about, do you know what books you were looking at, or, if you don't remember, where you were looking?"

Order thought on this, then nodded. "Order was looking in this book over here." She wiped the tears from her eyes and waddled over to an open book on the floor. It was an old,

leather bound tome with gilded tooling. The page edges were
tattered and slightly browned. She retrieved it, brought it back
to Abby, and handed it to her. Abby placed a finger in the book
to save the spot, then turned to the front cover.

Garathonymous Garrel's Book of Glyphs.

"Glyphs..." Abby wondered out loud. "In the back of my
mind I recall stories. But only whispers of memories remain.
Order, surely you were onto something?"

The dragon sniffled again. "Order doesn't know."

"Oh, I'm sorry. I didn't mean...I was just...never mind. Let's
learn together then, shall we?"

Order smiled. Together they turned to the first page. It read,
*"Glyphs are...objects of great power created by the combination of
a Fragment of Power, the soul of a being, and an instance of great
emotion...when you get near them you can hear whispers, ethereal echoes of power incarnate. Like lost souls have been drawn
to these objects, trying to find their way back to the realm of the
living through them..."*

Abby looked to Order. "Did the being that took your abilities sound like this to you? Like a bunch of voices, or maybe
as the book says, souls?"

Order nodded. "Read on, please."

"Okay...*Fragments of Power can come from many things,
including Ancients, the death of a powerful being, or even some
places where magic accumulates naturally and then splits off due*

to entropy...Fragments of Power can eventually turn into Glyphs themselves, but need to find a host, and a reason to come into existence..."

Abby and Order exchanged glances. They were on to something. Abby then moved onto the page that Order had been reading before her visit from The Seeker. "Look, here are the descriptions of the known twenty-one Glyphs. Listen to some of these: *Blood Spear, Chrono Crypt, Doom Helmet and Trident, Galaxy Chains, Grim Gloves, Helix Cannon, Negation Net.* These names sound incredible...Listen to this one: *Obsidian Soulstone, a dazzling stone of obsidian that is imbued with the soul of a shadow eater. The stone is said to be a portent for souls, and simply being near it eats away at your soul until it is entirely consumed within the stone. Origin unknown.* Order...look at the illustration!"

The dragon caught her breath. On the page, drawn with brilliant ink and a delicate hand, was the very same gem that hung underneath the cloak of The Seeker.

"The Seeker *is* the Obsidian Soulstone!" Order yelled. "I know something again!"

Abby's smile brightened her entire face. "Yeah, you do! But how does taking a soul take a dragon's abilities?"

"That's easy for Order, every dragon knows that. Our abilities are our souls, and our souls are our abilities."

"So, that's why Query, and you, feel so empty inside after meeting the Soulstone. It makes so much sense! Oh," Abby saw the loss in Order's eyes. "Oh, we will get the Soulstone. We will get your abilities back. I promise. Don't worry."

"Thank you Abby. Order is happy."

"Now," Abby clapped her hands. "Do you have any information on Demura?"

"Demura? Order has never heard of Demura. Why does nice Abby want to learn—" Order let out a shriek of terror. Abby's hair was turning dark, her eyes black, weeping blood, and her fingers into razor-sharp claws.

"Because nice Abby is one and doesn't want to be!"

It had fallen into twilight when I returned from purchasing double the amount of candies I normally did for Order—she deserved it. I pulled one out for Bitey Door and watched him happily chomp it up. I went inside and I could tell almost immediately something was off. I say almost because it took a few seconds for Order to scamper up my body and sink her teeth into my arm. Even then it took me a few moments to comprehend what was happening.

Ancients, I hate getting bit.

"Order, what are you doing?" I shook my arm and flung her across the room. She sprang to her feet and growled at me. Something was obviously wrong with her. Order usually had beautiful amber colored eyes. Eyes like Verdurian sunsets. Now they were bottomless pits of black and devoid of the wonderful creature I once knew. Black, just like...

"Order, stop this! What has Tyranny done to you?" I still had the pouch of candies in my hand. I waved it in front of her like waving a ripe yurn in front of a domesticated Kerbnab. There was a moment, a fraction of a fraction of a moment, where I swore the old Order was back. She swatted the candies out of my hand and jumped at my face. I turned, grabbed her by the waist and held her down. For a little dragon, she was tenacious. I took my mauling as I reached behind in my pocket, brought out the binding cuffs and bound Order hand to foot. She wiggled wildly on the ground trying to get at me, but it was hopeless.

Somewhere, another monster lurked.

"Come out, Tyranny!"

I didn't have an extra pair of binding cuffs, and as we've seen, my fighting ability was moderate at best. Not sure what I was going to do but I was ready to do it. Outside the Library of Order creatures began to gather. Either they were lookie-loos or heavily invested in the town's educational institutions. I didn't know. By their appearance I'd say the former, rather than the latter. Well, maybe the townsfolk did care because when they got closer, they at once turned to me and anger flared in their eyes. I mean they were practically foaming at the mouth, like I just punched their mother, livid. They also had the same, black obsidian eyes Order had. But despite her vehemence for tearing my face off, these people—for the moment—left me more or less alone. All it meant was Tyranny had called for backup.

"Tyranny, you coward, come and face me!"

Sharp claws raked across my spine. I hissed as pain splashed across my back. I spun, swinging my arm to strike, but she was gone. Another slash and I stumbled forward. Another hit, then another. The floor became slick with my blood as more of it poured from my back. My scales did nothing to protect me. Every time she struck me with her claws, more wounds opened, more blood wept forth. Every time I swung at her, I struck her shadow. It was like fighting The Seeker all over again. Pretty soon my back was in ribbons. The towns-creatures came shambling in. They didn't attack, but they spread out, forming a thick ring at least three people deep, blocking any chance of my escape.

"Tyranny...Abby...stop! I know you're in there!" I was coughing up blood now. Her slashes were going deep, deeper than I thought. "Abby, I know you can hear me!" I yelled with everything I had left. She walked behind me, raised both of her clawed hands, and plunged them down into my back and out the other side. She raised me up like an obscene trophy for all to see.

"Abby is gone. There is only Tyranny!" She threw me hard to the ground and I bounced like a ragdoll. I coughed and sputtered what life I had left.

I couldn't understand it, the last time we'd fought, we were somewhat equally matched, but now she was faster and stronger. I couldn't fight her, I couldn't keep up. Yet, I couldn't lose. I needed to save Abby. I needed to save Order. I needed to stop The Seeker. I couldn't lose.

I propped myself up on an elbow, then another. I began to crawl, dragging my body across the floor. To where and for what ultimate purpose, I don't know, but I crawled. My last act in this world may have been seen as an act of cowardice by some, but for me, it was an act of defiance. If Tyranny was going to kill me, she would have to do it herself and not let time do her dirty work for her.

"Where are you going, Query?" She walked up as I crawled. My answer nothing but throaty gurgles. I tilted my head to see her. I glared into her lifeless eyes, but reality set in and I knew I was done. She raised her clawed hand and with a blood-curdling scream, brought it down with brutal efficiency.

Life left me, and Death took me.

10

THE SON AND
THE SUN

A blood drop from the tip of the Demura's fingers hung frozen in mid air.

Time had stopped.

The moment was captured like a photograph. The dead eyes of the crowd, the victorious howling of Tyranny, the dead corpse of Query lying in his own blood. Everything was stopped in the moment except for Chronicle. The Valkyr, with her book open, stepped through the crowd as if none existed. To her, they didn't, not then. They were merely objects, obstacles in her way. She stepped over Order, whose face still held her wrath and contempt for the dead dragon.

There, lying in the middle of the room was Query. His back was torn to shreds from the claws of the Demura. His blood pooled underneath, like a macabre background to the painting of his death. Chronicle knelt, taking copious notes. Notes the dead dragon would never see, never read.

A book of infinite pages. Infinite stories, infinite lives.

"Yes, I know..." she spoke to the hushed whisper in her ear. "It wasn't his time. His job is not yet complete."

Chronicle rested her hand on his body. There was no heartbeat, no rise and fall of his chest. Query had truly gone to Expirius, the realm of the dead. But his job wasn't finished, the Ancient had whispered to her. He was still needed.

Chronicle closed her eyes. "Wake up, son of Genesis."

Query's eyes flashed open, milky white and dead.

The tattoos on her body glowed. Her other hand touched one on her upper shoulder, and as she spoke the words in her mind, the tattoo blazed with light. Magical power flowed from Chronicle and filled Query with new life. Slowly, his back knit itself back together. Flesh melded with flesh, sinew and cord strung itself again. His body filled with new blood. Hardened scales covered his wounds. It was like a decomposing body but in reverse. With each passing moment his strength grew more and more. Query returned to the realm of the living.

"Where am I?" he asked, his voice raspy and dry.

Chronicle looked at him as if looking at a newborn. "You are between the 'was' and 'will be.'"

"What does that mean?" Query got up on his elbows and looked at the scene around him frozen in time.

Chronicle shrugged. "I don't feel like explaining it."

"Oh."

"They," the Valkyr pointed at Tyranny and Order, "learned the truth about The Seeker, while you were out buying candies."

"They weren't for me, if that's what you were implying."

"Exodus thinks you're important—needed to destroy The Seeker. I don't agree."

Query sat up. "Chronicle, why are you telling me this?"

"Your job isn't to destroy The Seeker, it's to free her." Chronicle pointed to Tyranny. "You were right to question her. Why did The Seeker pick her to infect with the Demuric affliction and turn her into...this abomination?"

"Why?"

"Because she is not a mere human. She is the daughter of Exodus. She is—"

"She's a Valkyr just like you!"

Chronicle nodded, her wings flapping slightly at the dragon's revelation. "She was Absolution, Valkyr of Justice, born on the planet of Divinia."

"Was? What happened? Why was she on Entropus?"

"That is not my story to tell."

Query shook his head. "I don't get it."

"That's why she needs you. You are the only one who knows what questions to ask. She is the only one who can answer them. She is the only one who can kill The Seeker. Can you do this?"

"Why her? Why is she the only one?"

"It doesn't matter now. Can you do this?"

"I-I-don't know how."

"There is only one power in Infinitus that is powerful enough to aid you. *He* does not give it to you freely. It will exact a heavy cost with its use, so only use it when you have to." Upon Query's chest Chronicle placed a shimmering gem cut in the shape of a sun. Inside raged a fire so intense, Query believed an actual star laid inside.

"I give to you the Obsidian Starstone, a magic Glyph so powerful, there are few who can wield it. Be careful with its use. "

The Starstone attached itself to Query's chest without need of pin or cord. It blazed and filled Query with new life.

"I have toyed with time far longer than I should have, but remember, this is the only time I can reverse your death, so make this next life count. Bring back Absolution, bring back the Valkyr, and stop The Seeker. Stop the coming of Paracyst! That is what *He* wants."

"Wait, what does that mean? Chronicle? What's a Paracyst?"

The Valkyr was gone and the passage of time began again.

11

TIME FOR AN
ASS KICKING

I rose from my premature death bed and gave that Demura an uppercut she'll never forget.

My fist slammed into her and sent her screaming across the disheveled room. The enthralled townsfolk snapped out of their...enthrallment. Order's jaw dropped as she gasped in wonderment.

I was alive, and I had a Demura to destroy.

Tyranny got back up and rushed at me. With a screech, she spun like a tornado with claws extended meaning to shred me to pieces, only mid-spin, things slowed. She slowed down to the point that I easily side-stepped out of the way and she spun right past me. The Obsidian Starstone had given me some ability to manipulate time. Even Order and the crowd moved in slow motion. Tyranny landed, screaming in anger at missing her target, she turned and met the full wrath of my fist again as I struck her in the chest, hopefully to knock the wind out of her, and some of the fight. As she fell back, I swore I saw

Tyranny and Abby separate, just for a moment, then form back together. Tyranny attacked stronger and faster than before, but it didn't matter because no matter what she tried, she was slower. Every hit I landed was harder, faster.

Vengeance and anger flashed through my veins. I wanted to destroy Tyranny, I wanted to see her splayed on the floor in her own blood like she had done to me, for what she had done to me, for what she had done to Order, and for what she was doing to Abby. Yet I had to remember, if I killed Tyranny, I killed Abby, and she was the key to end The Seeker. I easily dodged another attack and struck the Demura in the chest again and I saw the separation between her and Abby.

"*Do it again!*" Abby yelled.

I struck Tyranny twice square in the sternum. The Demura flew back farther, but Abby separated and stayed close.

"*Again!*" she cried.

Tyranny was swaying. The beatings were taking their toll. "Abby, if you can hear me, I can't risk killing her. I can't risk killing you!"

"You might have to!" Tyranny cackled.

No, I'm not losing you Abby...I'm not losing Absolution!

"I'm going to try something! Hold on!"

I ran over to Order and shoved a finger in her face. "Don't bite me." With a flick I undid the binding cuffs.

"Order is sorry! Order doesn't know what happened..."

"It's okay, just get these people out of here!" Order nodded and began herding the townsfolk out of the library.

"Abby! Get ready for one dandy of a punch." I braced myself, brought my hand up, and beckoned Tyranny. "Alright you black-eyed psychopath..."

The Demura raged in a fury of unintelligible expletives that would have made even me blush if I could understand them. She bared her dark fangs, clicked her razor claws, and tore at me with everything she had. If I messed this up, there was no telling how savaged I'd be again.

This was it. My last chance.

Tyranny leaped through the air directly at me, and as she came within striking distance, I yelled the only thing that came to mind. "I am Query, son of Genesis, wielder of the Obsidian Starstone! Kindly...*get fucked*!"

I unleashed the power of the Obsidian Starstone and my fist transformed into a fiery comet as I drove it into the Demura's chest. I felt the pain of my wrist bones shattering under the pressure. The separation between Tyranny and Abby occurred again, this time more than ever. As Tyranny flew back from the punch, Abby disconnected and flew forward. Her arms went up, just enough that I quickly snapped my binding cuff around her wrist. When I had her, I pulled as hard as I could, while kicking Tyranny away. As I mentioned before, the binding cuffs don't just physically bind, but they bind to the individual's essence. It found Abby and held on tight. I pulled and pulled. There was an audible *snap* and she fell to the floor. I undid the binding cuffs and threw them in my back pocket.

"How...I saw you die?" Abby said as she got to her feet.

"I don't have time to explain, but you're actually the daughter of a dragon and are an angelic being known as a Valkyr."

"Wait, I'm a what? Why are you telling me if there's no time?"

"Sorry, there's no time! We need to deal with Tyranny!" But there was nothing left of the Demura. Not a trace.

"Is she dead?" I asked Abby, who was also looking around for her evil doppelgänger.

"No," came a small voice from behind them. "Order saw her flee."

"Makes sense," Abby replied. "I can still feel her. Whether she is near or not, I don't know." Abby rushed to the little dragon. "Oh, Order, I'm so sorry I made you do those awful things. Are you okay?"

She nodded. "Order knows it wasn't nice Abby that did those things, it was mean Tyranny."

"Yeah, Order." I added. "You pack quite a punch for a little dragon. I won't be messing with you any time soon."

By now my arm was killing me. I winced when I tried to move it.

"Nice Abby, Query is hurt."

"I see that. We need to get him to a hospital, then he can tell us why he is alive, what a Valkyr is, and what that pretty thing is on his chest."

"I suppose we have a lot of catching up to do, but the longer we wait, the more dragons will become ghosts and lose their abilities."

Abby shook her head. "There is nothing we can do about that until we catch up and put all of our information together. Plus, going after The Seeker *and* Tyranny without a plan is suicide."

I couldn't deny she was right, as much as I hated it. I just knew that there were far worse abilities on Adjura for The Seeker to take that would only make our jobs at stopping it that much harder.

The Seeker wasn't a person but a thing—an object. I'm a talking dragon so I wasn't too surprised. The Glyph was called the Obsidian Soulstone. It possessed a host and now was calling itself The Seeker. Yes, the similarity in name to the one I wore on my chest wasn't lost on me and now I have a new fear to worry about. Wonderful.

We went to the nearest hospital, which wasn't near at all. The Library of Order wasn't that close to any major cities. So we had to take the tram, which was actually the root system of gigantic trees with movable cars inside. At least they didn't bite. The longer I stayed on Adjura, the more I had come to appreciate its weirdness, and the more I wanted to save it from The Seeker, and whoever, or whatever this Paracyst was. To be honest, it sounded more like a skin condition than a person.

While I got treated for multiple wrist fractures and burns—I have dragon scales, so the fact that I was burned at all tells you how hot my arm got—Abby, Order, and I discussed everything we knew. Now that we knew *what* The Seeker was, it made sense *why* it was doing what it was doing and *how* it was doing it. We knew *where* it was—somewhere on Adjura, hopefully. All that remained was *when* it would strike next. That's a lot of questions answered and for me, a weight lifted off my shoulders. There of course was another *how* question that needed answering. How do we stop a sentient Glyph?

According to Chronicle, that wasn't my problem, that was Abby's. This was her domain. It was my job to convince her she was one of the divine Valkyr. My first plan was the simplest. I just told her.

"No, no way," Abby replied, shaking her head.

Okay, so much for the direct approach.

"Why else would The Seeker pick you to turn into a Demura? Why not Tim?"

Poor Tim.

"I don't know, we don't even know what a Demura is."

"I've fought one, several times. I could pick one out of a crowd."

Abby shook her head. "No, you know what just one looks like, you don't know what one is. It has to do with the bite, I'll bet every last credit I own on it. Can The Seeker change anyone into a Demura?"

I didn't know.

"Until we do, that isn't enough to prove I'm divine."

I was running out of options, not that I had too many in the first place. "What about your dagger?"

"What about it?"

"Don't you think that dagger looks awfully Valkyr-ish?"

"I don't know what that means."

"Oh come on!" I winced as the doctor worked on my arm. Evidently the doctor thought dragons didn't need painkillers. "Never mind." That's when I thought of Order.

"Order, you're unusually quiet. What do you think?"

"Order doesn't think," and she started crying.

"Oh, right. Sorry." Then I had an idea. "Order, can you help me out?"

That stopped the crying. "Yes, Order will help."

"Can you go back to the Library and see what you can find on the Demura and Valkyr and have it sent to me?"

She nodded. "Yes, Order will do that for you friend, Query."

I smiled. It was good to have Order back. "Thank you my friend, now fly, fly like the wings of a dragon!"

Abby cocked her eyebrow at me. Oh no, the doctor *did* give me painkillers. No wonder I felt so...nice.

"Query?"

"Yes, pretty lady?" I started getting sleepy.

"Dammit, Query! Stay with me. Where is he going to go next? Tell me where he is going next?"

My eyes were closing. "Fierce. I bet my cute little behind he's going after Fierce." I performed a little dance, then fell directly asleep.

"Query?" She shook my shoulders, but I was out.

12

CANDIES FOR QUERY

I awoke the next morning. My head felt like Feast sat atop it dining on three courses all at once. If you don't know about the dragon named Feast, he's a big ol' boy and usually in a good mood as long as you bring snacks. Lots of snacks.

Abby sat in the corner of the hospital room, slumped back, resting her head against the wall. She must have stayed with me all night. I didn't expect that. I guess I assumed that all the talk about the Valkyr would have scared her off.

Guess I was wrong. I'm glad I was.

"Hey, good morning sleepy head," Abby said when she noticed me staring at her.

"Shh...not so loud." My head pulsed with pain.

Abby sat up. "I whispered that."

"I know, your whisper is so loud."

"How's the arm?"

"It's fine. It'll hurt for a while I'm sure."

Abby stood and walked to the edge of the hospital bed, which had also just woken up and was relieving itself. She placed a comforting hand on my upper arm. "The doctor said that the cast they gave you is strong enough to protect it and keep all your bones in place, but you shouldn't be fighting again."

"Well that sucks."

She smiled at me. "You said last night that The Seeker would be going after the dragon, Fierce, next. Why?"

"Huh?" I was still pretty groggy. "Fierce...oh, yeah. Fierce is, well...her tenacity is beyond measure. Her ability to strike fear in the hearts of her enemies is so powerful, they are left paralyzed in their own hopeless despair."

"Wow, you're quite eloquent when you've been doped up."

I shrugged.

"I don't get it, The Seeker is already incredibly powerful, what's stopping it from doing what it wants to now?"

I smiled at her, at least I think I smiled. I might have still been drugged up. "You're right, the Obsidian Soulstone is already powerful, but even all-powerful Glyphs have their limitations. Case in point." I hold up my broken arm as evidence. "Also, it has lost its number one bodyguard. For all we know, it's us versus a rock."

"Then we need to get going!" Abby jogged to the door. "I'll grab the doc and get us out of here."

"Wait, wait." I held a hand up to her. "I don't know about you, but I'm really tired of not having a plan, *and* being one step behind."

"But Fierce?"

"Fierce is likely already gone...there is nothing we can do about that now. However, once The Seeker has all the dragon souls it wants from Adjura, the only place left to go is Separas, unless it plans on backtracking, which I highly doubt. No, it's going to Separas, home to some of the most powerful dragons ever. Their abilities negate the abilities of other dragons. They're a pain in the ass to fight, and I try to avoid them at all costs, but..."

"But what?"

"But we're going to have to play nice and get them to fight alongside us. Convincing them will be about as easy as convincing you that you're a Valkyr."

Abby scowled. "I'm not."

"Yes, exactly."

After a morning meal and a visit from the doctor, we were cleared to leave. Actually, we weren't cleared to leave, but when Abby insisted we be allowed to go, and then the doctor inexplicably caved, we left. I brought the fact up to her that people did as she said, even when it went against their better judgment, and how that wasn't normal, but she didn't want to hear any of it.

Maybe I needed a new tactic? Maybe it was pointless?

We prepared to leave when a scurrying sound came up behind us. It was Order, come to see us off. We exchanged goodbyes and Order even had a present for me as a way of apology.

I held the bag of candies in my hand. "You know this isn't necessary. I know you were enthralled."

"Order knows, but Order still feels bad. Look inside. Order got your favorite!"

"I don't eat—" but she had already moved on to Abby, saying her goodbyes.

Abby, for her part, gave Order a giant hug. "We'll be back as soon as we can. I promise you. You've been a huge help Order. I'll forever be in your debt." This made Order giggle and tear up, but the little dragon was resolute. I looked into the bag of candies, but instead of sweets inside, I found a folded up piece of paper. Carefully, I drew it out and unfolded it. What I saw took my breath away, and I knew in that instant that I could never show Abby. Not until she was ready. I folded it back up and tucked it into the bag. "You're right, Order. These are my favorite candies. Thank you. We gotta get going now."

"Order heard that The Seeker has reached as far south as Purge."

I smiled. "Perfect, we will have some time. Abby, are you ready to go?"

She nodded.

I grabbed her close with one arm—the other was in a sling. She held on tightly and I could feel her warmth. Not of her body heat, but another kind of energy. Kindness. I hoped she could feel it too.

My wings unfurled.

The ground trembled.

The pebbles rose.

The world was silent.

We shot off like a rocket.

We landed on Separas in the late evening. At least I think it was late evening. As mentioned, Separas is perpetually dark, save for the white flashes of light due to its proximity to The Loop. That and the deathly silence. I forget how unsettling it can be for a human. There aren't many on Separas, and the few that did hang around live in the cities inside the magical dead zones that allow for speech and sight. Otherwise, the atmosphere was suffocating, like the bottom of the ocean. Of the four dragons here, I landed among the desolate temples of Banish, inside yet another one of these dead zones. If anyone could help us stop the Obsidian Soulstone and The Seeker, it would be him.

He was a priest. Not in the traditional sense of a leader of congregations, but in the sense that he was a wielder of holy magic, a healer, and kind of a dick. But most importantly, Banish was obsessed with the ushering of the dead into the realm of Exile. It was his passion, his life's calling. Some called him a zealot. I called him a self-righteous tool.

However, his ability is exactly what we need him for. Maybe he can exile the souls inside the gem, or the gem itself...what does that mean for the other dragon's powers...I don't know. I'm winging this. But if anyone knew what to do about this damn Glyph, it'd be Banish. So here we were, a dragon and a self-denying Valkyr climbing the eight hundred steps of the pyramidal temple of Banish. High amongst the clouds. At the top, the dragon would be sitting under a stone canopy, in the prayer position, constantly ushering the dead into Exile. When we actually got to the top, that wasn't what we saw. Instead of the almighty Banish...

"Oh no, not you..."

13

THEM PEARLY WHITES

"Hello, little Query."

Oh grunk!

"Omega, what's new?"

Standing at the top of the temple in all her glory, was the bipedal red dragon, Omega, sister to the dragons Alpha and Delta. They're buff and dumb. At least one of them is dumb. I can't remember which. I think the green one. She, however, isn't. Omega does not suffer fools and in her mind's eye, I'm one of the biggest fools in Infinitus.

"I hear you are on another one of your quests. And you're failing." She looked down at me. Omega's only a foot taller than I am, yet she makes a big deal in calling me little.

"You're right, I'm a professional that calls missions, *quests*. Where's Banish? We need to talk to that religious nut-job."

Omega folded her arms over the glistening ruby embedded in her armor chest plates. "Query, why am I here?"

I scoffed. "Because you're awesome at being a pain in my ass?"

"Because The Seeker is wreaking havoc and you can't stop it."

"And what are you going to do? Karate-chop it to death? Seriously, how did you find out?"

"It doesn't matter." She took a step past me and eyed Abby. "You're not Valkyr."

"Yes, thank you!" Abby let out a big sigh. "I've been trying to tell him that. Please tell him that!"

"Not anymore," Omega added.

"Oh, come on! What is with you dragons?" Abby turned and took a seat on the stone steps.

Omega shook her head and returned her stare back on me. What a joy it was to have the eyes of that dragon on you. I mean, seriously. Nothing but warmth.

"Omega, where is Banish? We need him," I said.

Her eyes narrowed. "I sent Banish away for his own safety. Why do you need him?"

Seriously, with the questions! "We need him to try and exile The Seeker. This is the next planet it's coming to."

"Is The Seeker dead?" Omega asked.

"What?"

"Dead. Is The Seeker dead?"

I shook my head. "No. Why?"

Omega gave me the look of *oh you poor, poor idiot.* "Then Banish won't help you. He only exiles that which is already dead. If The Seeker isn't already dead, he can't exile and your plan is over before it began."

Dammit.

"Dammit!"

Omega spread her hands out. "Little Query, you're not thinking! Banish can't exile...but I can!"

She's right, I wasn't thinking. I was too upset about being wrong. Omega and I were from the same home planet. Omegaia. Yeah, if you caught that her name is in the planet name, you weren't hallucinating. It is. Having to live up to someone like that is tough. Not that I tried.

"Query! Are you listening?"

"Of course!"

Okay fine, I totally tried. I tried really hard, but Omega is smart, beautiful, and deadly. The worst part, if you don't live up to her impossible standards, she'll let you know about it.

She glared at me. "Then what did I say?"

Guess what, I have never met her impossible standards and she has let me know it every day I've ever had to deal with her. Again, why she is here, I wish I knew. I'd strangle whoever told her to within an inch of their life...

"You said you were sorry for how you treated me all these years and you'd like to make it up to me. Also, you can send others to Exile. See, I was listening."

Omega grunted. "Fine."

"But it isn't going to help you."

Omega and I looked down at Abby sitting on the steps looking out over the rolling clouds.

"Why is that?" Omega asked, but I already knew the answer.

Abby got off the step and turned around, now looking up at the towering Omega. "Because you can't get near it. If you do for any amount of time, the Obsidian Soulstone has got you. If you want to fight The Seeker, you're now going to be fighting nine other dragons' abilities. You won't be able to exile. You won't be able to do anything." Abby turned back around and took her spot on the steps. "It's hopeless. The Seeker is going to continue to suck the souls from dragons and take their abilities and no dragon can stop it."

"Then why would Exodus give this quest to me?"

Omega smirked. "Knew it was a quest."

"Shut up, I'm being serious! What's the point if it's futile?"

Omega looked down at Abby, "because we aren't the ones to stop it, she is, isn't she?"

I got mad. Madder than I should have. I have many regrets. This is one of them.

"Yeah, she is, but she is too block-headed to have an open mind about it."

Abby turned around. "It isn't about having an open mind, you dim-witted dragon! It's like trying to convince you that you're human! No matter what I said, there is no way you'd believe me! So what's the point?"

"The point is, I was told when I died that I needed to convince you that you were a daughter of Exodus—"

"You died?" Omega asked.

I ignored her. "Convince you that you were a Valkyr, and if I can't, then The Seeker wins and Paracyst comes to Infinitus and nobody tells me what the hell a Paracyst is and now Red here is on my case for failing! What am I supposed to do? Now if you'll excuse me, I'm pissed off because out of this entire screwed-up cluster, Abby you were the one who has had my side the entire time and I need a minute!"

I started to descend the eight hundred steps of the temple into the gray mists that shrouded the bottom. "Nobody follow me!"

"You're not a child, little Query!" I heard Omega shout. "Stop acting like one!"

"Shut up! Not everyone gives a grunk what you think!" And then I was lost in the mists.

You know, I'd like to think I don't lose my cool that often, but man was I pissed. The last thing I needed was to have

Omega stick her snout where it didn't belong. I didn't need her help, I didn't want her help, I didn't ask for her help. I'd kill whoever told her. Probably Chronicle. The Valkyr were driving me nuts lately. First Abby being so stubborn, then Chronicle following me without even having the courtesy of telling me that she was following me down the stairs. I could hear the scratching of her quill and wet ink against paper right now.

"What do you want, Chronicle?"

More scratching, wet noises. Like the sound of a tongue scraping the roof of a mouth.

"Chronicle, dammit I'm talking to you!"

Scratch. Scratch. Scratch.

"Chronicle I swear if you don't say a word in the next five seconds I'm going to lose it and you can write that down in your stupid—"

Something screamed and attached itself to my face. I swatted it off, then another one landed on my shoulder. I could feel strong teeth. I swatted that one away easily just as two more let out a peal of sound and landed on my back. The yelling grew to a terrifying crescendo as more and more bit down on me. I swatted them away in a frenzy but I could feel their teeth getting under my scales. Realization set it and I ran for my life back up steps to Abby and Omega. I had only heard about them, infesting the depths of Banish's temples, but never seen one, let alone thousands, in real life. I burst through the clouds and into the darkness of Separas screaming at the top of my lungs. "Chompers!"

Imagine skin covered balls with human teeth and long, thin tongues. Hideous things. Pitifully easy to deal with one. Deadly in large numbers.

I could see Abby looking down at me in confusion. Omega quickly got into fighting position, a blue ethereal blade in each hand.

"Are those Phantom Blades?" Abby asked. "I recognize them from Order's book."

Omega gave Abby a wink.

Like a wave, the Chompers rolled through the cloud and skittered in the thousands up the temple steps. Abby had her dagger in her hand. I never saw her get it out.

"Move out of the way!" Omega yelled.

I dove to the side just as Omega flew, literally flew like a magenta fury down the stairs, blades out, and crashed into the onslaught of Chompers, exploding into them like a cannonball into a ship. She landed in fighting position and brutally stabbed everything that moved. Teeth shattered and tongues went flying. Seeing Omega work is a rare treat. Like watching any expert working their craft, Omega's was fighting. The way she moved. The violence, the carnage.

It was glorious.

I turned to Abby, holding the dagger like a sword. "I thought you didn't know how to use that."

"I don't, but I don't want to be eaten either."

"Fair enough. Come on, get these things off me!"

Omega was overwhelmed. Despite her prowess in battle, she could only do so much to the growing number of Chompers. Once I was cleaned off, Abby and I raced down the stairs, flailing our arms and legs trying not to fall. A far cry from Omega's entrance. We made it in time to remove twenty or so that had attached themselves over her body. More flew our way and Abby batted them away with her dagger like it was sport.

"Thank you," Omega yelled. "But, this isn't your fight. You two need to go and stop The Seeker!"

"But, I thought you were—"

"Shut up and go!" Omega spun and plunged a Phantom Blade straight through a chomper and into the stone step as if it were butter. "Don't worry, I called for backup."

"Abby, let's go." I grabbed her by the wrist and led her around to the other, and hopefully chomper-less, side of the temple.

"Wait, what did she mean by backup?"

Two shooting stars streaked across the midnight sky. One a brilliant sapphire, the other, a verdant emerald.

"Don't worry about it," I said to Abby. "It just means the whole place is about to get a lot dumber."

14

OF LOSS AND
REMEMBRANCE

We ran.

We ran from the Chompers. Great explosions of violence and laughter erupted behind us. If only we had that courage, or stupidity, to laugh at such danger. Omega and her brothers would be fine. They'd been in far worse. For Abby and I, it was a nightmare. For them this was fun.

Good for them.

The trip back to civilization gave us a lot of awkward time to spend together once the threat of Chompers had left. From what I've heard, they don't like to leave their home nest.

"Abby, look, I'm sorry. I didn't mean to call you a block-head."

"It's okay."

No, it wasn't okay.

"No, it's not okay. Actually, I did mean to call you that, but I didn't mean to be such a goblin's ass about it. Why are you so resistant?"

"I'm sorry, I just...you haven't shown me any proof yet."

I was silent for a while as we trudged through the thick jungle that ringed the temple. Then I remembered. I did have proof. I took out the bag that Order gave me and extracted the piece of paper.

"I didn't know when I was going to give this to you. Maybe I should have done it right away, but deep down I knew that this wouldn't be easy. Guess maybe I was trying to spare you from pain." I handed the paper to her. "This is why." In the dim light of The Loop, it was still clear what it was. The ruby pendant that Abby wore around her neck.

"Order gave this to me. It says your necklace is a Glyph, an item of extreme power. The Traitor's Mark. It's cursed. It has the ability to hide a true form, and in some cases, remove memory. Abby, you're either in extreme denial, hiding something from me, or you truly have no idea what's going on. Whatever the pendant is hiding, though, it isn't good."

Abby let out a long sigh through pursed lips. Sweat dripped down her forehead.

"Tell him," came a voice.

I could feel her presence before seeing her. Maybe we had a connection now that she had brought me back from Death.

Great.

"Chronicle, give her a minute," I pleaded.

From behind the thick jungle brush Chronicle appeared. Her wings folded tightly behind her, her eyes piercing white. "She doesn't deserve a minute."

I looked at Abby. My heart beat faster, for I knew what was about to happen would not be pretty. "What is she talking about?"

"I...don't know!" She shrugged, looking to me for answers I didn't have. "I've never seen this person in my life!"

Chronicle took a step closer. "I'm your sister!" she yelled. For the first time I saw true emotion come from the Valkyr. "We are blood!"

"I-I'm sorry, I don't know you."

"Okay. Let's take a moment here." I raised my hand in between the two, "Abby, the thing around your neck is affecting your memory. The only way we can move on is to remove it. I can take the Traitor's Mark off for you, if you'd like," I offered.

"You can't!" Chronicle said. "It is a cursed item. Only she can remove it."

"Abby." I tried to be as gentle as possible. "Take off the pendant and then we, all of us can finally see the truth. I promise you, I won't judge."

She looked me in the eyes. I thought she was about to tell me no, and use her persuasive nature on me to get me to agree, but she didn't. Instead, she gave a quick, tentative nod. Abby slowly reached behind her neck and undid the clasp. Off came the pendant and she handed it to me.

At first nothing happened. I thought maybe I'd been wrong. Maybe this was just a regular piece of jewelry and Abby was just Abby, but then, she looked upon the Valkyr with the quill and book with brand new eyes.

"Chronicle...Query...I...oh...by the Ancients...I remember. I remember everything now." Abby burst into tears and collapsed into the fresh loam of the jungle floor. She heaved heavy sighs as she wept. I turned to Chronicle for guidance, but she only took a few notes in her stupid book and watched. I knelt down to place a hand on her back but as I did, two great wings sprouted, knocking me backwards. I crawled away. She was Valkyr alright, she even glowed with a golden aura, and right now she appeared like a fallen angel. I had never seen something so breathtaking, yet so sad in all my life. I knelt down by her side and asked her again once the weeping subsided.

"Absolution?" I asked.

A final, heavy shudder racked her body. She looked into my eyes. "Query, you were right."

"Tell me. Tell me what happened."

Golden tears ran down her cheeks, dropping silently into her palms. "My...my children..."

"You're a mother?" I asked. The way she comforted those around her—of course she was.

She nodded. "Yes, two beautiful daughters. One I named Truth and the other Solace." She held her arms as if she cradled them. "They were my babies. Even when they grew older and wiser, they were still my babies. The two of them did everything together. They were inseparable—we were inseparable. I love them so much. Loved them."

"Loved?" I asked. "Absolu–Abby, where are they now? Where are Truth and Solace?"

The tears rolled down her cheeks again. "They're...gone."

"Gone? Gone where?"

"Dead," Chronicle said coldly.

I looked at Chronicle, then back at Abby. "Dead? Dead how?"

Absolution shuddered. Her hands were shaking. "Solace was...Solace was taken by a Demura. The same kind that The Seeker used on me. Only this time, she didn't have a dragon to save her." A faint smile briefly graced her face at that. "When she fully turned, she called herself Anguish, and anguish was all that she gave. She kidnapped her sister, tortured her, and..." Absolution's eyes closed, pressing out the pain. "And eventually killed her. Truth's last breath was a curse on Anguish, a curse so powerful that it created that." She pointed to the pendant in my hand. "The Traitor's Mark. Originally, it was a gift from Truth to Solace, now it is a symbol of Anguish's betrayal.

"When I found out what happened...well, there are no words to describe the grief a mother feels at the loss of a child. Or the anger that rages through a mother's veins at the person responsible. What does a mother do, though, when the person responsible for killing your child...is your child?"

I shook my head. "I can't even fathom."

Her face grew sour. "I hunted down Anguish and ended her life. I didn't even think twice. I am the Valkyr of Justice and I took my own child's life." She let out a deep breath. "I took the pendant as the last memory of my children. I learned that if I wore it, I wouldn't think about them anymore. I didn't think about the pain. I was no longer Absolution the Valkyr, I was Abby, the bartender on Entropus, and in my ignorance, I was happy again."

"Yet, you left us; you left me," Chronicle said. "How could you leave me? We were friends. We were sisters!"

Absolution turned to her sister. "We still are, I just didn't know how to deal with all this then, or now. Honestly, I don't know if I ever will." She turned back to me and held out her hand. I hesitated. I didn't know the right thing to do. In the end, it wasn't my place to decide what to do, it was hers.

"Please, Query."

I handed the pendant back to her. She clasped it around her neck. The glow dimmed and her wings faded into nothingness. She was Abby the barkeep once again. I looked around and

Chronicle had vanished. I didn't blame her. This was heavy stuff to deal with and I can't say I blamed Abby for wanting to live in ignorant bliss. And I didn't blame Chronicle either. Feeling disowned by someone you love... I just can't imagine. It made me think about me and my dragon brethren. We weren't close at all. And that's when sadness overtook me. I was envious of the anger Chronicle felt about losing Abby, because one thing is for sure, if I left Infinitus, not one dragon would give two grunks about it. So that begs the question: why am I fighting for them when Abby has been the closest thing to family for me since we met?

"Hey, aren't you a super magical interplanetary space dragon? Can't you fly us out of this place and back to civilization?" Abby said, her faculties returned.

"Technically, if I were to fly *within* the planet that would make me an *intra*planetary... you know what? Never mind. Sure, let's get outta here."

Why am I fighting for the dragons? I'm not.

I'm fighting for her.

15

EMPLOYEE
DISCOUNT

There was still one question that wasn't answered. Why?

Why was The Seeker doing this? Sure there was the obvious "why" of just *seeking* to gain power (see what I did there). Dragons are the most powerful creatures in Infinitus. Let's pretend for a moment that The Seeker was going to sap the abilities of every dragon. Every single dragon. That's a lot of dragons and if I was going to fail at every turn, that was going to make for a very boring story and I don't like those. I can't believe that that is what The Seeker is doing. Case in point, it went to Omegaia to steal the abilities of Peek, just to be able to teleport its way across Infinitus to attack Null? And completely ignore Omega?

Come on.

There is definitely some method to the madness and some grand scheme. Unfortunately, this personified Glyph is incredibly terrible at monologuing its plan. It's a real pain.

"Who's left on the planet?" Abby had asked.

Void was a psychopathic monstrosity who wanted nothing but to destroy the world. Seems tempting to a power hungry megalomaniac, but we just established that it isn't likely that is what The Seeker is. If you've ever had the displeasure of meeting Void, you'd figure out pretty quickly that he is also a power hungry megalomaniac, and you just can't have two in the same place.

Another dragon possibility was Fade. But The Seeker could have Fade for all I cared. I'm not dealing with that weirdo.

"That's your reasoning?" Abby said as she sat across from me at the diner as we ate breakfast. "Fade is weird?"

"I'm telling you. I talked to her at a party once, she showed up in my dreams for the next three weeks just wanting to hang out. It's like, hey, just call me."

Abby took a bite of her flumpcakes.

"Think about it. The only place from here to go is back to Adjura, which, why would it do that, or—and I bet my credits on this—the Obsidian Soulstone is headed for The Loop. That's why we need to meet with Cancel. Nobody knows the Loop's magic like Cancel, and if we can make sure that he is still on our side and hasn't lost his powers to The Seeker, then we are one step ahead."

"Alright, you're sure about this?"

I nodded.

"And do you know where to find Cancel?"

I laughed. "Heh, do I know where to find Cancel..."

I had no clue where to find Cancel.

"You have no clue where to find Cancel, do you?"

"Alright, we've been hanging around each other for too long. Here's the thing with Cancel. He can't really see, or hear, and he can change color at will so..."

Abby tossed her fork down. "And this is a planet of perpetual night. Hey, I have a better idea, let's go back and fight the Chompers. That'll be more fun than trying to find this camouflaged, deaf and blind dragon."

"It's not impossible, it just won't be easy."

"Query! You're talking about finding a single dragon on an entire planet! Where do we even start?"

I looked around. "Here I guess." I stood up and cleared my throat. "Hey, has anyone seen a color-changing dragon named Cancel anywhere?"

"Yeah, he works in the back!" someone yelled.

Abby and I immediately locked eyes. In a rush, we got up from our seats and worked our way into the back of the diner. Sure enough, the dragon was back there working the grill.

"Cancel?"

The little dragon turned and chirped at me, his skin flashing in a dazzling array of colors. I think he was happy. I hoped at least. He can get kinda testy if my memory serves.

"Cancel, it's Query. We gotta go! Big trouble! Come on!"
Even though he was blind and deaf, he still could fully understand what was going on through fluctuations in the quantum
matrix. Whatever that meant. I was told at a party but I think
I was trying to avoid Fade. The little dragon chirped again,
undid his apron and threw it on the floor.

"Where're you going? You still got three hours left on your
shift!" a portly man in a stained shirt yelled.

Cancel chirped something that I don't think should be re-
peated and followed us out. I threw the man some credits for
the trouble, which seemed to appease him some. We left the
diner, and I made the formal introductions.

"Dude, what are you doing working a grill?" I asked. "You're
a damn dragon!"

Cancel vehemently chirped and grew animated.

Abby looked concerned. "What's he saying?"

"Um, basically he said that his existence has lost all meaning
and time is but an endless burden of nothingness that led to
the loss of hope and worth as a being in the eternal cycle that
is the infinite."

She was taken aback. "Oh...oh my."

"And he really liked the employee discount."

Then I told him the story from Exodus to now, leaving out
the part of Abby and her Valkyr-hood. I'd let him figure it out
later. He mentioned that he had heard something about The

Seeker and had hoped to lay low and out of sight, and thanked me for now dragging him into it.

Sarcastic little...

But in the end, he understood his crucial part to play. We needed to get to The Loop. But the universe never just lets us do what we want, does it?

We happened to be in a city called Geddos. A motley crew of two Dragons and a "human" walking down the busy streets. Again, nothing terribly out of the ordinary. However, something was off. I could feel it. Abby could feel it. Even Cancel was chirping incessantly in my ear. I looked around and saw concern on the faces of those around me. Some not just concern, but fear, and some who I made eye contact with, anger.

"Abby, you're seeing this, right?"

"Oh yeah, I'm suddenly not feeling welcome."

"I don't think it's you. I think it's Cancel and I."

"Why do you say that?" she said, not breaking stride.

A Planarian waddled by and glurped, "Eat grunk, dragons!"

"Ah."

I grabbed the arm of the next passerby. "Hey, what's going on?"

They ripped their arm out of my grasp and with a hiss said, "you should know, idiot."

"Well I don't, moron. Tell me!"

"Xeresis City is under attack!"

"By the Ancients...The Seeker?"

"What's a Seeker? Dragons. Dragons are attacking Xeresis City!" The passerby shouted an expletive and continued on. Abby and I ran through the streets. Cancel took flight and soared over our heads. It wasn't the greatest of ideas as this caused screams from pedestrians. It did open the way for us quite nicely. We raced until we found a large holoscreen attached to one of the buildings playing a news report. Footage from Xeresis City showed utter devastation. The dead were lying everywhere. Dragons swept the ebony sky raining hellfire down upon the innocent below. Why would they do this? Then I realized, they wouldn't. The Seeker would. The camera panned to the left and I found my answer. Coiled in the sky was Chaos. One of the four dragons taken on Entropus. The Seeker was using Chaos's abilities to turn the powerless dragons into its army. They may have lost their magic, but they were still dragons and dragons were still formidable.

"Cancel!" I yelled up at the color-shifting dragon. "Get to The Loop and hide. Wait for us there. Don't let The Seeker find you!" Cancel chirped and off he rocketed to The Loop.

I'd see him soon. One way or another, I'd see him soon.

"Abby, we need to get to Xeresis City. Come on...oh grunk."

The camera panned again. This time another dragon appeared. I had been wrong. The bastard did it anyway.

The Seeker went after Void, the power hungry megalomaniac.

And The Seeker won.

16

BATTLE OF XERESIS CITY

Xeresis City was a crumbling mess of mayhem and havoc, a battlefield. It was eerie to see the fire of dragon's breath yet hear nothing because of the magic in Separas's atmosphere, despite the wind and heat of fire whipping around us. Creatures ran but we heard no screams until we were practically on top of them. High in the sky the dragons flew, raining down their fury. It was the most awesome display of their power I had ever seen. And these were dragons neutered of their powers.

These were just dragons being dragons.

"Hey you dick-heads, knock it off!" I yelled, but my words melted inches away from my mouth. This was hopeless.

"*You* knock it off," Abby scolded. "That won't do anything." She observed the carnage surrounding her, "Is there anything we *can* do? Even if we get their attention, would they even stop for us?"

"I haven't any clue, Chaos's abilities are incredibly persuasive, so much so he can even compel betrayal." A few moments thought and it dawned on me. "This is The Seeker's final move. It has to be. The Obsidian Soulstone's final play. It's making for The Loop, and this is the distraction."

Abby agreed. "That means *we* have to make for The Loop!"

I turned and a giant flaming boulder hurtled through the blackened sky. In its path a helpless bystander stood frozen in terror. I couldn't see who it was and it didn't matter. I ran as fast as I could, but I wasn't going to make it in time. The person was scared out of their mind. I yelled for them to move, but they couldn't hear me. The fireball was within a yard or two of striking. With one last push off my feet, my wings unfurled and I blasted through the air scooping them up in my arms just as the boulder smashed against the ground, cratering the spot where we were moments before. I skidded to a halt as the fire singed the tips of my wings.

"You?" they said.

I looked at the person in my arms and started laughing, despite the chaos. "I told you I would find you."

Cradled in my arms, was Jova, the Gorgian. At least I hoped it was. She probably wished she still had the rock coming at her. She struggled to get out of my grip.

"Wait, don't go." I said, "actually, I need you. Are you still arms dealing?"

She cocked a spiky-fishy eyebrow at me. "I gave that up. I'm legit now."

"I'm not hauling you in. I promise. Now seriously, are you still arms dealing?"

A fireball flew past our heads and struck the ground a few feet away. "Fine, yes of course I am! Why?" We were losing time.

"Then I need lasers. Big lasers! Now!"

She nodded. We grabbed Abby on the way and ran to Jova's stash. It was four blocks away in the storage compartment of her transport ship. It was slow going, climbing over bits of rubble and fallen buildings, dodging hellfire and trying to stay out of sight of the other dragons. Now was not the time to be noticed and spat upon. We made it to the ship. Jova searched for the keys to the storage compartment.

"Come on!"

"Hey!" she snapped, "that doesn't help!"

"Sorry."

She found the key, and opened the trunk.

"Wow," I said, looking over her inventory, "you sure love snazzium-plating." Every laser, of every shape and size, was there.

"These won't kill them," Jova said.

"I'm not looking to kill them, just get their attention and get their focus away from the city. Abby, grab whichever one looks good."

"Hey!" Jova put her hand in front of the merchandise. "These aren't free!"

"My loss of credits for not turning in your bounty paid for these. Does that sound fair?"

She eyed us both. "Yeah sure, fair."

I was about to choose my weapon when I heard a whistling in the air. I looked up expecting another fireball, but watched as a blue, green, and red missile landed in three heavy thumps right behind us, kicking up dust all around us. I thought we were ground-zero for a bombardment, but as the dust cleared, three shapes coalesced into the three mighty visages of Omega and her brothers Alpha and Delta.

"Don't think you can have fun without us, little Query." Omega smiled, and for once in my life, I was incredibly happy to see that smile. Happy to see her alive. Happy to see dragons on our side.

"Step right up, they're free. Today only."

Omega put a hand on my shoulder in greeting, then went to the trunk and took out a plasma machine laser. The blue sapphire colored Alpha did the same and picked another formidable weapon. The emerald scaled, golden horned Delta, ever the charmer, punched my arm, and after a thorough search, picked up a weapon that was deep in the back of the storage compartment.

"Is this what I think it is?" he asked, eyes gleaming at the intricately designed green hammer.

"Oh, you know that's not a laser, right?" Jova said.

"Delta, get a shooting weapon for Ancient's sake," Alpha pleaded, his eyes still fixed on his own laser rifle. "We're after *flying* dragons."

"I'm taking it!" Delta took it and measured its heft. "Feels good."

"What are you going to do with that, brother?" Alpha asked with a jealous sneer. "Wave it in their face?"

Omega's jaw hung open. "Fool! Don't you realize what that is? That's the–"

"Whatever. Let's go." I said. I had had enough of them already. Man, I have zero patience for these three.

We marched into the open crater of the city. Like heroes marching into battle. Well, actually, we were marching into battle. I had no idea if what we were about to do was going to work but we were going to look really cool doing it.

"Find some cover," I told them. "And when I give the signal, unleash hell."

"What's the signal?" Abby asked.

An emerald blur whizzed by me, screaming something completely unintelligible. Up it rose into the sky and in a majestic arc, swung the maul. A shockwave of thunder rippled through the silence of Separas and a bolt of white lightning leaped from the weapon right into the roaring face of Chaos.

"Yep, that'll do."

The remaining four of us let loose a salvo of fire from our snazzium-plated weapons. A rainbow of colors poured forth from our lasers up into the sky, harassing the dragons that harassed the city. Lights of brilliant golds, oranges, reds, blues, and magentas reflected back on our faces.

By the Ancients we looked amazing.

The smoldering edifice of Extinct broke through the atmosphere and threatened to swallow us. We turned and focused our fire straight into her incoming snout. It was enough to turn her away.

Whatever we were doing was working as the dragons attacking left the city alone and focused on us. That also meant we were losing, as we dodged fire and debris. No longer could we stand in place, so we scattered like fish in a pond. My place of cover was getting pelted, I was close to getting a face full of fire. Alpha was across the crater, beckoning me to come to him. I nodded and took off running. Halfway there, something hard slammed me into the ground, knocking the air out of me. My laser flew out of my hand leaving me weaponless, save for the Obsidian Starstone, something I didn't want to use unless absolutely necessary.

"You can't stop us, Query. Xeresis City is ours!"

I looked to the sound of the nasally voice and saw what had crashed into me. Overhaul, the cybernetic-suited dragon from Entropus.

"Yes, it is I, Overha—" A magenta blast took him off his feet and sent him flying into nearby rubble.

Alpha came up and extended a hand. I eagerly took it.

"I hate that guy," he said.

Omega ran up to us "The three of us can handle these dragons, you and Abby need to get after The Seeker. It's going for The Loop isn't it?"

"We think so, yes." I looked around. "Where's Delta?"

Omega pointed up. I followed her finger and saw him riding the back of Chaos, bashing the great dragon on the back of the head with this hammer.

"He'll be occupied for quite a while," she said. "Go, we'll be fine."

"Why? Why do you suddenly believe in me?"

Omega gave me a look, one I've never seen from her before. Respect possibly? "Let's just say I had a good talk with someone who has your back. Now, I've got it too." Behind her, Alpha nodded.

Chronicle. Maybe she's alright after all.

"Thank you. I won't forget this."

The two siblings smiled and went off to continue to fight. "Hey, I saw your laser shoots magenta," Omega said to Alpha as they walked off. "Mine shoots blue. Wanna switch?"

So on brand.

I turn to Abby. "We're going to The Loop, but I can't carry you there."

She didn't understand at first, but then she did. She touched the Traitor's Mark Glyph she wore around her neck, the one that hid her true form.

"But I'm not..."

I held her shoulders. "You are, you know you are, deep down, you know there is something more to you. I need the warrior. I need you, and you need Absolution."

She looked down at her feet. "You're right, there is something inside me, and I can't fight it any longer. I have to become what I am." She looked up at me, her eyes two pools of black void. Blood ran down her cheeks. "I am Tyranny, your end!"

"What—"

Her laser fired into my side, and once again I was dying.

17

THE LOOP

The Demura whispered as life ebbed from my body. "You see, dragon, the Traitor's Mark hindered me, arrested my normal Demuric metamorphosis, but I've since learned to overcome it. I've learned to work against the Mark. You didn't destroy me in the Library. I simply made you think you did."

Oh Ancients...

"I bided my time. You know, illusory magic is so underrated, don't you think?" She walked a circle around me as I stood in shock. "People love fire and transformation, but look at everything that I did to make you think you'd won." Tyranny stopped behind me and whispered in my ear. "You can't separate a Demura from its Valkyr, Query. We are one and the same. Your Abby is gone. Tyranny remains. Enjoy the sweet embrace of Death."

An evil cackling rose from her lips and she flew off. Slowly, I slumped to the ground. I reached for my side and felt the hole the laser had left. The plasma it discharged created a fist-sized crater in my side. Luckily–if there was a luckily–the plasma cauterized the wound, so at least I wasn't going to bleed to death. Dragons are incredibly hard to kill, but this'll do it. The wonder triplets were out fighting. I could hear their cries of laughter as their onslaught continued. I tried to scream but nothing came out. My lungs refused to fill all the way. My body splayed out on the ground and there I laid. There was no telling for how long. Eons could have passed and I wouldn't have known. I couldn't count on Chronicle coming to heal me again, and this was beyond the magic of the Starstone.

Dammit, I'd lost. We'd lost. Infinitus lost.

Worst of all, the realm lost Abby, and that I just couldn't allow.

I propped myself up on my elbow, gritted my teeth through the pain, and held my side as I rolled over onto my belly. My strength fled me. Every second I waited I would become weaker. Every second more The Seeker and that damn Glyph were going to bring down my home and I wasn't going to let that happen without a fight. I sucked in what little breath I had and pushed myself up. I curled a leg underneath me, then another. Slowly I got to my feet, pain surged throughout my body and I threatened to fall again. I told it to shut up and do as it was told. I stood upright, the battle of Separas raged around me. I looked up to The Loop, the brilliant blue orb of light made of pure magical energy. Somewhere up there was The Seeker and Tyranny. Pretty soon, it was going to have me.

I spread my legs, unfurled my wings, dug deep, and found every ounce of energy I could muster. The ground around me shook as the primordial essence of my draconic flight took hold. Rubble around me rose in preparation of the shift in gravity. It froze, then slammed violently to the ground as I slingshotted out of the planet's gravity well and into space. The flicker of colors around me flashed. I had no time to appreciate the experience. The only thing on my mind was Tyranny. She was going to pay for what she did to Abby.

The Loop got larger and larger in my field of view. It grew with my anger. It grew with my ferocity. It grew with my hate for The Seeker. My pain was nothing but a distraction. My dying, nothing but a side effect. My life was nothing, merely a preparation for this moment.

There, with its arms raised, blaspheming the sanctity of The Loop's magic, was The Seeker. Above it, a vortex of blackness swirled like an ebony whirlpool.

Void.

The Obsidian Soulstone was opening a black hole inside the Loop using Void's powers. It was going to destroy the Loop!

"Stop! You destroy The Loop, you'll destroy Infinitus, you'll destroy us all!"

The Seeker continued, paying no attention to me.

"You stupid Glyph! Knock it—" A force struck me from behind causing me to spin wildly. My wings outstretched, stopping the spin. Tyranny laughed. She hadn't lost any of her potency now that we weren't on solid ground. Abby had fully turned Demuric. Whether she was still there, somewhere, I had no idea. The amount of strength she must have used up just to stave off the inevitable...

She came at me, the light of The Loop reflecting off her claws. I tried to dodge, but was too slow. Tyranny slashed her claws against me and sliced through my hard dragon scales. She pivoted and slashed again, then again. I was back in the Library of Order, only this time I was wounded from the beginning. She came back again, but I was ready. This time, I remembered the powers of Genesis, the Starstone. Time slowed to a crawl and I got out of the way, but strength still drained from me and even with my time advantage, I barely got away in time. She passed me and I struck her with my busted arm, the one still in the special cast from Adjura. She turned with a new ferocity and howled with a new attack. Time slowed, I dodged, and struck. We did this dance three more times until my strikes were nothing more than tickles. I couldn't move anymore. She sensed this and renewed her vigor. Slashing and screaming at me, I held the cast up as my only defense. Beyond her, The Seeker conjured its dark magic, the black hole growing ever larger.

"Stop you fool, you'll destroy everything!"

"Join your voice with mine, child. Together we will sing the lament of Infinitus and the coming of Paracyst!"

"I don't give a grunk who Paracyst is! Stop!"

"You will!" the chorus cried.

The Seeker increased its power and the chorus chanted:

> "*Othbana...thalna...keelga...Paracysta!*"
> "*Othbana...thalna...keelga...Paracysta!*"
> "*Othbana...thalna...keelga...Paracysta!*"

Tyranny dug her claws into me. I knew this feeling. It was familiar. It was Death. I felt it before in the Library of Order. There would be no one to save me this time. If I was going down, so was the Demura. I knew Abby was in there somewhere and I wasn't going to let her be tortured like this. There was only one thing that could be done now. One thing left for me to do. With the little strength I had left, I brought my arm back, revved up the Obsidian Starstone, and for the second time in my lifetime, I gave that twisted Demura an uppercut she'll never forget.

My arm became ablaze with stellar power, my cast shattered, and all of my might went into that strike. It wasn't much, but enough that Tyranny was thrown away from me in an arc with blood splattering into space.

I got her. I got her. And she got me.

The last thing I saw before dying were two glowing eyes staring out of the black hole, and a glint of red floating around Tyranny's body.

Abby came to me in a dream.

Not the Abby I once knew, but Absolution. The Valkyr. She was wearing golden armor. Her pristine white wings floated behind her, upon her head was a golden helm. She was ready for war. No, she was ready for justice. She radiated life, warmth, and light. She was beautiful.

I was wrong, she *was* the Abby I knew.

"Thank you, Query. You have found your absolution, and so have I."

I realized the Traitor's Mark was no longer around her neck. In her hand was a brilliant sword, its blade made of light, its hilt bejeweled. Her hand was on my chest.

"Rest easy now. Your job is done," she said to me and was gone. I still felt her warmth on my chest.

I was floating on my back. I tilted my head and The Seeker was still there, opening the black hole. I could not tell anymore what was real or dream. I looked down, which for everyone else was up, and there, set against a backdrop of a million stars, was a golden rocket, streaking across the sky, wings tucked in, sword held forward, battle cry echoing throughout The Loop. Behind her, an army of dragons. Omega, Delta, and Alpha. Chaos, Overhaul, Extinct... even the gigantic Void was there, all letting loose their salvos of hellfire upon the black hole. Absolution let out another battle cry and the dragons sounded as one. They flew over me. Tears rolled down my cheeks. I had never seen such a sight before. The Seeker held up a hand, and I could feel its nullification magic from where I was, I could feel it trying to engage every one of the dragons' abilities it had stolen. None of The Seeker's magic worked. From behind it, Cancel appeared, undoing everything the Obsidian Soulstone attempted to do. Cancel opened his jaws and bit into the head of The Seeker, shaking it violently and tearing the cloak completely off, exposing the Obsidian Soulstone.

The Valkyr are warriors, they don't need to rely on magic. The Seeker never accounted for a warrior of Divinia caring about the realm of Infinitus. Absolution dove blade first into the exposed Soulstone. It penetrated the ebony gem and shattered it into pieces. Shards flew out in every direction and lit up like diamonds against the light of The Loop. What was left of The Seeker evaporated into a cloud of dust and was no more. The entity in the black hole unleashed a cry of defeat, the hole closed in on itself, then winked out of existence.

I fell back to sleep, and my dream was over.

18

Q & A

I woke up.

I woke up laying in the rubble of Separas.

I woke up to the faces of my family.

Dragons.

"He's waking up!" someone yelled.

I blinked as the consciousness took hold. My side ached, but I reached over and felt no wounds.

"How?" I grumbled.

"Shhh..." It was Abby's voice. I looked over but it wasn't Abby. She was dark, with golden spells woven throughout her skin, and she was staring down at me.

"Crokinole? Is that you?"

"Chronicle. Yes, it's me. How are you feeling?"

"Like I got run over. Did I get run over? Did somebody get the ship's registration plate?"

She smiled at me. "We're still gonna get you to a hospital, but I have a feeling you're going to be just fine."

"How?" My voice was still a dry rasp.

Chronicle winked. "I'm not the only Valkyr with the power to heal."

I looked around. "Where's Abby?"

"There he is!" I felt a hard slap on my chest. "How are you feeling, Little Query?"

I shut my eyes and smiled. "You know I hate it when you call me that, Omega."

"Well, it's a term of endearment," the ruby dragon said. "We did it. We won!"

I looked at her. "It wasn't a dream?"

Omega nodded over to Chronicle. She reached inside her leather bag and extracted shards of the once Obsidian Soulstone. It didn't look so dangerous after all, just hunks of rock that no longer shined in the light.

"Where is Abby? She okay?"

Chronicle and Omega exchanged looks. "Abby needed to leave, but she says she'll see you again. Said you'll know where."

I did.

I spent a cycle in the hospital in Separas. The dragons that could fit through the door came to visit me. They braved a city that now had every right to despise them, just to see how I was doing. Even Order left her Library to see me. Brought me a lot of candies too. She sat with me awhile, telling me more about Valkyr, Glyphs, Demura, everything. Some things that would have helped out days ago, but hey, better late than never.

Omega, Alpha, and Delta visited. They had returned their weapons, except for Delta who kept what turned out to be a Glyph of immense power, the Vortex Maul. He said, and I quote, "you can have it when you rip it from my cold, dead, perfectly sculpted hand." Banish, the nut-case even came to visit when he'd heard what was going on. Omega sent him on vacation and he had no idea whatsoever anything was happening.

Chronicle came several times to visit. One was to confiscate the Starstone. I was sorry to see it go, but I was done having all that power. She asked questions about my side of the story, and I did my best to answer. You know, she's alright. She even brought me a magical deck of cards, just like my old one. Yeah, she's alright.

As for the city, despite knowing the full story after the fact, and understanding the dragons were under a spell from The Seeker, they still kept a healthy wariness of our kind and Xeresis City leveled a ban on all dragons in the city.

All except for me.

I left the hospital and went to the place I knew where I could find Abby. I'm an interplanetary space dragon, I'm sure I've mentioned that, but this time, I took a ship. Just didn't have it in me to fly. Not alone.

I landed near a little town called Sea'd on the planet Entropus, one of twelve planets of Infinitus. A quaint little sea-side village of hearty people. It was evening. The planet's moons hung high in the sky. It was the kind of place I would want to live when I retired. If I retired. I'm not ready yet. Still plenty of bounties out there and credits for the taking. I sat at the edge of the cliff, looking out on the ocean, the sweet smell of salt filling my nostrils. I still had my Demura upper-cutting arm in a sling. Thanks to the power of the Starstone, it'd take many, many cycles to heal.

I heard a light thump behind me. I smiled, already knowing who it was. I turned and there stood the winged figure of Absolution. But underneath the golden aura, the golden armor, and the golden crown, was Abby. The armor melted away, the wings tucked themselves in, and the aura vanished. She came and sat next to me on the cliff.

We didn't speak. There was nothing to say at first, just the company of each other was all we needed. The time that had passed since the Loop had been far too long, but now it was like she had never left my side. No words were needed, just her presence, her proximity, her friendship.

I noticed a white diamond pendant around her neck. She must have caught me looking.

"It's magic," she said, finally breaking the silence. "Chronicle gave it to me. Look, if you hold it up to the light..."

She took it off and handed it to me. I held it up into the moonlight. Dimly there, but still visible, like a hologram, were two girls, smiling and holding each other in an embrace.

"Is that who I think it is?"

Abby nodded. I handed the treasure back to her.

Now was time to ask the question that needed to be asked. "Why didn't you stay for me? After, I mean."

She looked out over the ocean as if it held the answer. "I'm sorry I left you. There were a lot of emotions I had to deal with. Killing your best friend for a second time is something I am still working through."

I turned toward her. "Yet you didn't, Tyranny did. I know the difference between the two."

That seemed to perk her up. "Good."

"And hey, you saved the world in the end. You did it!"

"No, we did it."

I nodded. "We did it."

Both our eyes gazed back over the sea. For a time we just sat in each other's company again, talking of things that had nothing to do with The Seeker, the Obsidian Soulstone, or anything that had befallen in the past cycles. The night grew darker until the stars of Infinitus came to life and sparkled their light across the black satin sea. Finally, as all things must, it had to end. She stood and returned to the full glory of her Valkyr form once more.

"Query," tears welled in her eyes. "I have to go. I have to return to Divinia, sort some things out. I don't know when I'll be back."

I nodded. "It's okay; I understand." It wasn't okay and I didn't understand. I couldn't be without her.

We stared at each other, neither of us wanted to ruin the moment. Neither of us wanted the moment to end.

She took a few steps back. I knew what was coming next.

Take off.

Someone had to do it, why not me? "Goodbye Abby. We'll see each other again. I promise we will."

"You're right," she said. "I promise too. We will see each other again."

I smiled. I couldn't help feeling like somehow, we wouldn't.

She took a few more steps backwards. Her wings flexed out and flapped a few times, sending gusts of wind into my face. She crouched, thrust all power into her legs, but didn't move. She remained on the ground, held fast by a force neither of us could see, but both could easily feel. Our connection held us together. Abby looked into my eyes and I looked into hers. She rushed to me and embraced me.

"Come with me," she said, whispering into my ear. "Come with me to Divinia. Let's fly together."

I pulled away. "I can't, you know I can't. I..."

Over Abby's shoulder was a little girl I hadn't noticed before. She stood in the shadows of night, not fifty feet away from us. She dressed in rags, hair whipping in non-existent wind. I knew who the child was without question. She gave me a smile and nodded her head.

I looked Abby in the eye. "Abby, let's go to Divinia!"

My wings unfurled.

The ground trembled.

The pebbles rose.

The world was silent.

We shot off like rockets into the moonlit night sky.

Together, as we should be. Exodus promised me rewards. I can't think of any greater treasure than this.

THE
CONUNDRUM
OF THE
SOULSTONE

"Tell me again how he did it."

The Valkyr sighed. "The power of the Starstone broke the Demura's infection on Abby and Query broke the cursed necklace holding the Traitor's Mark, releasing its power over Abby. Absolution took over and fought with the dragons and destroyed the Obsidian Soulstone. After the Soulstone shattered, all the souls were released, and all the dragons got their abilities back."

"Hmm...I was right to pick him," the Ancient mused.

Chronicle sat with her book open, her quill sat in an inkwell ready for its use. At the workbench, tools of every magical kind lay strewn about as well as several shards of black stone, while other larger shards were put back together in its original form.

"Are you sure you can do this?"

"I'm sure as long as I'm not bothered," Chronicle huffed. "It's just like a puzzle."

She often referenced her book with the original image of the jewel. It was old, ancient, like the one commissioning the project.

Slowly, one by one, the pieces fit together. A bit of magic held them together and sealed the seams. It looked like nothing happened at all, like a Valkyr with immense power hadn't destroyed it. Chronicle worked hard under intense scrutiny. This was a delicate operation. Even the tiniest shard needed to be put in its correct place. The project has been going on for three days now. Three days of no food, no rest, no stopping. Bit by bit, piece by piece, it came together.

The Obsidian Soulstone was coming back to life.

"Are you sure about this?"

"Yes, continue working."

It was the fourth day. "Exodus...you better get in here!"

A specter of the ancient appeared in Chronicle's workshop.

"What, what's wrong?"

"Look!"

Chronicle pointed to the stone, and a pristine tabletop. The stone was missing several chunks.

"We didn't get all of them."

Exodus looked at Chronicle with fire in her eyes.

"That means someone else got them."

"What do we do now?"

"We pray they are on our side."

Excerpts from Chronicle's Compendium of Infinitus: Dragons

Alpha – 10ft 6in. A bipedal dragon with large toned muscles and striking blue armor. Honor and ideals are of utmost importance to him. Generally means well, but may not always go about it the best way.

Banish – 6ft 6in. A thin bipedal dragon with dark bat-like wings. Generally wears a jewelry adorned headpiece and minimal cloth wraps. A true zealot of the dead, Banish is priest-like in his devotion to stopping undeath, and will go to incredible lengths to ensure no creature commits such unholy acts.

Cancel – 4ft. 6in. A small dragon with thin bright wings and a carapace that is spiked around the limb joints. His skin generally has a bright blue hue. This little dragon has been rather difficult to study, as he lives on a planet with no light or sound. The Loop's energy seems to course through his veins, allowing him to change color at will - a very useful camouflage or distraction tactic. Cannot see or hear, but senses others through heat and quantum disturbance. Truly an interesting creature.

Chaos – 36ft. long, 12ft. high. A massive serpentine wormhole dragon with rippling gold and orange scales. This dragon is well... chaotic. He does not seem to care for society or structure in general, and actively seeks to sow discord into such notions. Incredibly difficult to trust, as he will intentionally ruin everything at the worst possible moment to cause as much confusion as possible.

Coax - 2ft. 4in. A tiny serpentine dragon with an array of greenish scales that change color based on lighting. One of the smallest and quickest dragons in the realm, Coax uses her size to great advantage. Nearly impossible to catch due to her size, speed, and iridescent scales which confuse the eye. Very quick witted and sharp-tongued.

Delta – 9ft. 4in. A very muscular dragon with brilliant green armor. Is more brawn than brains, and doesn't seem to have an issue with it. Often doesn't understand the consequences of his brash actions. Can often be found working out or training with heavy weaponry.

Exodus – 8ft. 8in. A bipedal dragon with elegant and ornate armor. One of the four Ancient dragons that created Infinitus. She wields the powers of order and logic, and has the omnipotence to see and feel great imbalances in the universe. As one of the Ancients, she is rarely seen by mortals, if ever. Some claim to have had her visit them in the dream realm, but many of these claims are unverifiable.

Extinct — 40ft 4in. A giant meteor dragon. Generally spends her time orbiting Entropus, and appears to travel using some sort of telekinetic levitation.

Fade — 3ft. 8in. A small teal colored bipedal dragon with a tail protruding from her head. A very curious little creature. Speaks very cryptically much of the time, but seems to be wise in a way that others simply don't understand. Has a unique connection to the Exile through her mastery of The Loop. Because of this, she has the ability to enter the dreams of others, as well as influence them.

Feast — 13ft. 0in. Rotund, with yellow scales and orange spines. A voracious and insatiable dragon that is nearly as round as he is tall. Food is his primary motivation, as he is always hungry, and therefore driven to continuously consume.

Fierce — 6ft. 1in. Smallish, with red and charcoal scales. Despite being a rather small dragon in terms of stature, the abilities granted to her by The Loop allow her to paralyze her enemies for a short period, stopping them from mounting an effective attack or defense. Unfortunately this ability does nothing to stop the magic of other dragon's abilities, but regardless makes her a very effective ally on the field of battle.

Genesis — 8ft. 8in. A bipedal dragon with regal armor and reflective red wings. The Ancient of time itself. Legends speak of his prowess as a battlefield general, but few have seen hint of him for many ages. There do exist rumors that he has been pivotally involved in a few more recent conflicts, appearing as a common highborn soldier, but no irrefutable evidence has been unearthed during my studies.

Null — 21ft. 11in. A menacing serpent-like dragon that radiates a magical blue aura. Quite a powerful creature, with an aura of magical silence that ensures battles involving this dragon will be decided by sheer might alone.

Omega — 8ft. 1in. A bipedal dragon with a harsh demeanor and utilitarian red armor. Stern, strict, and stoic. A master of martial arts and hand to hand combat. Also a very astute strategist and tactician.

Order — 4ft. 4in. A very studious dragon with the appearance of a woodland creature. Has brown and white fur rather than scales. Rather particular in her ways, but generally quite amiable to interact with. Has a vast wealth of knowledge about most topics in the universe.

Overhaul — 5ft. 3in. Bipedal, with a cybernetic dull grayish-blue suit of armor. A rather annoying dragon, with a nasally voice that has a prominent way of irritating nearly anyone. A useful ally for sure, but constantly brags and seeks attention, making for horrible company.

Peek — 2ft. 8in. A dragon with fire red eyes and steel colored skin and scales. A particularly small dragon, which lends benefit to his wily nature. His ability to travel through small wormholes makes him top-notch at spycraft.

Purge — 34ft. 9in. Vulture-like in appearance, long-necked with massive leathery wings. A very large dragon that thrives on taking advantage of change. Rather than try to embed herself in the machinations that exist, she will take advantage of the uncertainty brought about by a change in the status quo.

Query — 7ft. 5in. Bipedal, with dark blue scales that have an oily reflection. A bounty hunter dragon with excellent tracking capabilities and a grasp of magic that allows him to see between realms to glean information on any creature's whereabouts. He is persistent and determined when put to the chase, and rarely fails to capture a foe.

Void — ?ft. ?in. Variable in size and shape, generally with an ultraviolet and indigo hue. Void is a hellish creature that is psychotically bent on rending a hole in the universe and evaporating all matter within it. Can create black holes. This is an extremely dangerous ability and this dragon should not be overlooked for long periods due to his destructive nature.

Acknowledgements

This book came about in probably the most serendipitous way possible, and for that I am forever thankful. I had expected Theo to seriously talk about it in the foreword, but instead he went insane. It's okay, I can use that word because I too am insane.

In truth, I actually didn't think I would get another book completed this year (2025) and yet here you are, holding another creation. Thank you, the reader, for taking a chance on a card game novelization (first of it's kind? I can't think of a single card game, not even a famous one created in 1993, that has it's own novelization) that really had no right to exist. Had it not been for a little Minnesota convention where I was introduced to the game, Scale: Rise of Dragons, and its creators, this book certainly wouldn't have happened.

Many thanks to Theo Stai, the main facilitator and lore master to the world of Scale whose knowledge has been invaluable in the making of this book. Seriously, there is a reason I asked him to write the foreward. He even wrote the Excerpts from

Chronicle's Compendium and many other bits of lore found in the book. We spent many hours going over the ins and outs of Infinitus. Basically, no Theo, no book.

Thanks to Kevin Botts for creating the amazing game in the first place. Thanks to everyone else at Upscale Games for not only allowing me to play in the world you created, but being able to make part of it mine.

As always, many thanks to the trusted readers who went through every page and gauged this book's worthiness. Most were cool with it, thank God. Alla, Em, Hannah, Katherine, Robin, S.J., big thanks!

To my coffeeshop friends for the constant encouragement and my family for putting up with my constant anxiety, you will always have my undying thanks and love.

Lastly, thank you Ancients, for not eviscerating me and feeding me to the rotbirds!

ABOUT THE
AUTHOR

Ian Young is a human writer who has lived in the Twin Cities, Minnesota, for most of his life. When not writing, you'll find him hanging out at the local coffee shop, playing board games with his spawn, or working in his garage wood shop. His debut novel, The Automaton, won the 2023 Best Indie Book Award (BIBA) for science fiction, and is a Book Readers Appreciation Group (indieBRAG) medallion honoree. His follow up, Ashen Light, is also an indieBRAG medallion honoree and a Readers' Choice 5-Star Read. You can connect with him on Instagram @ianyoungwrites.

"*The Seeker has failed us? A pity it had no flesh left to punish. So be it, let the Dragon and the Valkyr celebrate their ill-gotten victory. Oh yes! Yes, my winged pretties... Yes, you mustn't need to worry, you'll be consumed soon enough.*

If Divinia wants to play in our game, then we, I, me, shall play in theirs.

The foolish fleshed Infinites believe they have won, but even a sliver, delivered precisely, will stop a beating heart. A heart that we shall devour, divinely. Run along now little Spawn of Infernus, and tell Death that I suppose we would indeed like to bargain, after all..."

– Oracle of Dream Vol. 7: Viewing 8
Cycle 8, Revolution 8, 4175